THE POLE AND WHISTLE

BY

GEORGE MOOR

THE POLE AND WHISTLE

BY

GEORGE MOOR

SOLAR PRESS

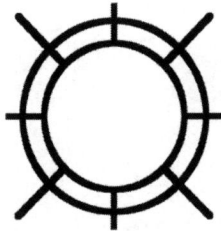

Second Solar Press Printing

2023

Originally published 1967

ISBN: 978-1-7393532-6-1

Printed and bound in England by Imprint Digital Exeter

For inquiries and information please email: info@SolarPressBooks.com
Or visit: www.SolarPressBooks.com

CHAPTER ONE

I was desperately thirsty, tired and alone. It was a long walk to the flat, and after going without sleep for thirty hours I wanted just to lean back and close my eyes. I saw the lit curtains and the bright glass inner door of The Pole and Whistle and so for the first time since I began working at Barraclough's I did not go straight home.

Since I was in the sixth form at the grammar school I had scarcely gone drinking in pubs. Certainly it had never occurred to me to walk into one alone. I wondered at myself now for trudging home night after night all these years with such a thirst when a means of refreshment so simply presented itself. Over the door was a board showing that Alfred Shaw was legally empowered to sell intoxicating drinks and cigarettes, inside was a small uneven mosaic pavement worn by the traffic of inward feet. I saw the word 'welcome' in the design as I drew the glass inner door towards me and it closed at my back with a rubber-muted thud.

It was a shabby pub inside. If it had been a matter of conscious resolve and decision, perhaps I would have gone into one of the smarter hotels in Hawkward. The White Lion put on expensive evening meals, advertised a cocktail lounge and was patronised by the local Rotarians. As it was, chance or my stars had halted my feet at the nondescript Pole and Whistle, set back from the main square as if to escape notice. The place was of some antiquity, I knew. In the ancient documents of Hawkward it figured as The Polecat and Weasel, but the original name had gradually grown to its present form. There was nothing old-world about the interior, which was too featureless to be called with any truth Victorian, so I assumed that the present structure merely occupied the site of the old Polecat and Weasel and retained the glory of the name.

The bar-room was less a bar-room than an enlarged corridor. In the cramped space three men stood drinking—one very tall slumped on his elbow, another very tiny with his hair growing over his collar. Surveyed from the back the three looked like an ascending chord. The three of them shot looks at me, and the barman gazed my way. He had a mild, friendly expression but was heftily built. There was a gold flicker in his smile and his black hair was rather extravagantly creamed and moulded. As he moved to fetch me a lager—for not knowing the brewery I ordered the first bottled drink which I could see—I noticed that he was becoming a little portly and wore a sober English suit of very good cloth.

"Would you like lime with it?" he asked, advising me that lager by itself tended to be insipid. From his gentle friendly voice and unforced pleasantness I had the instant conviction that here was a genuine and good man. There was more here than just a professional nice manner—with his service he seemed to give something from his full human self.

Some stools were ranged around an old iron table and there I retreated with my gold-rimmed lager glass. I had hung my umbrella over the top of a thin flat radiator against which I leant, the warmth blowing drowsily on the back of my head as I listened to the men in the bar talking. The little man with the long hair spoke hardly at all, but solemnly supped his drink. He was Irish and named John. The big dark man was called Norman, drove a lorry and betted on horses. The elderly man in between these two was not addressed by name and contributed to the conversation old evidences from his experience. The man behind the bar was called Alf and I took it that he was the Alfred Shaw named as licensee outside. Now and then a buzzer would sound and in a bell-board hung to the side of the bar a marker would joggle excitedly, summoning Alf to service in other rooms of the pub. Three doors led from the narrow bar-room, presumably to the various rooms named on the board. There was a sport's room, from which I could hear the thud of darts, a 'parlour' which I took to be the empty room with black leather seats that I could see through an open door, and a 'singing room' from which no singing came, but into which, every now and then, Alf carried drinks through the door on my left.

I sat drinking in pleasant drowsiness, reading the advertisements and the labels of the bright decorative bottles on the shelves. The sporting conversation did not interest me at all, but I was aware of it going on. The middle man of the trio left, throwing us a good-night nod. The door gave its rubbery thud after him. I had my glass refilled. The lager had a soothing and also an enlivening effect on me, I became more and more immobile and rested while at the same time becoming more refreshed and awake, as if in a state of clear trance. No doubt I was not very joyous company. Other people, all men, came into the bar and I did not speak to them. From the singing room also young men would cross the bar-room on their way to the gents. Everybody seemed to speak to everybody else. I alone in their midst was a stranger.

I had spent most of my twenty-five years as in a railway carriage where no one spoke and everyone kept his reserve. More than fatigue and thirst, it was the loneliness that had withheld me from returning direct to the flat tonight. Yet it was only in loneliness that I could feel myself and be at ease. With any other human being I would have to be under constraint and the need to act a part. I could never be liberated from an inner watchfulness. To myself I disclosed only a slumbering awareness of what I was in the secret depths of being, and to others I had always striven to give no indication of my true nature. Thus I lowered my eyes like a nun whenever the young men in tight blue jeans passed through the bar-room from the singing-room to the toilet.

"Could we have some shillings, Alf?" one of these blue, jeaned young giants with a brush of golden hair hanging over his forehead, asked, coming up to the bar. "If it's connected."

"He came tonight," Alf replied. "Just a bit earlier on; I was waiting for Evelyn to come in and try it out. It's got her favourite disc."

"Walking back to happiness with yoo-oo-yoo," sang the strong wingless angel identifyingly and roaring the song out he danced into the singing-room with the shillings.

There was some scraping, a clatter and a boom and suddenly the building was caught in a lassoo of vibrant sound and beating rhythm.

"Twist again," a voice amplified sang out in command like the voice of God. "Round and round and round we go again."

There was a shriek from the singing-room where a chair overturned with a crash.

"It's a bit loud," said Alf mildly. "It'll need some adjusting."

After Chubby Checker came Elvis Presley, and then the disc of Helen Shapiro's "Walking Back To Happiness With Yoo-oo-oo-yoo." The electronic loudness of the juke-box like a hunting cry seemed to summon the pack of Hawkward's youth. The outer glass door had hardly thudded back before a new group of youths were swinging it open again and they would pass, bright-shirted, elaborately hair-styled, tight-jeaned, into the singing-room with its great shining Moloch of a juke-box.

The singing-room was very much the teenagers' province, I gathered. But even the older customers at the bar could not escape the hypnotic blare. I was now approaching my fifth lager. The swooning, erotic pulsation of the music and the love-sick elegiac lyrics had invaded my consciousness. Like a chameleon I changed my emotional colour with each succeeding song. I yearned for "Johnny" and I flamed for "Norman". I felt in low spirits about money with "Johnny Will" and I rose triumphant with "The Young Ones".

Alf's wife, Evelyn, had appeared like an elegant Maenad as soon as her favourite song came on the juke-box, her body swaying to the rhythm and her fingers snapping. Her hair was dyed honey-blonde; she wore a tight pale-green sweater and a pleated brown skirt. In her ears were cameo ear-rings, genuine ones from Italy I noticed from close scrutiny as she came before the light. She was a tall, attractive person with taste in her dress and make-up. One thing alone detracted from the favourable impression she made: her speech. I had seldom heard a more common and slurred intonation than hers; there was an adenoidal cast to all she said.

"How's it going, love?" she said to me, her hips swaying, as she brought me another lager and danced with a full tray into the singing-room. Norman's black eyes were directed on her quivering rear like blow-lamps. I could understand how someone as undulant and elegant as Evelyn, with her very light colouring and blue eyes innocent unto vacancy, must appeal to a Tarzan male like the lorry-driving Norman Povis. The peaceful Alf did not seem even to notice, let alone care about the *oeillades* glancing like gunfire between Norman and his wife.

When the juke-box first whooped up the invitation to 'Twist' it had brought the darts players out of the games-room. One of them, standing dart in hand, looked in age about twenty-eight. He stood there, smiling, tall and muscular. I noticed the smartly pressed black suit, the highly polished shoes, the clean-cut face and the glinting fair hair before he turned away. The sight of him disturbed me as if undraped Pan had momentarily appeared in the doorway of The Pole and Whistle.

I do not think he saw me then but later, returning from the toilet, I found no one at all in the bar except the darts player with an empty glass waiting before the taps. I returned to my umbrella on the radiator. As I drank my lager I felt that he was studying me. For a while I did not raise my eyes. When I did so my gaze met his in shock, like glass meeting a furnace-fire. I was unequal to the encounter; I was twisted and changed in structure and ran into new forms. Throughout my life I had disguised my true being, but in this collision of eyes I was revealed, exposed like a chick breaking through into the sun and a new atmosphere. At that moment I knew that he was the sun into which I would fall. In the dizzying pull out of orbit I did not notice what colour his eyes were. Only his voice came to me, pleasant and guarded in tone and mysterious as if we shared a secret. "You were on 'D' landing in Stafford, weren't you?"

"Stafford?" I echoed, brought again to outward reality by the surprising conspiratorial tone—and in a sudden inspiration I had it, as I remembered the one occasion on which I had been in Stafford. I was being taken in a car on some business for Barraclough's and the driver had had to make a detour which led past the rose-red brick walls of a very obvious prison.

"The prison?" I said, seeing that image of steel-doored landings so familiar to me from the quantities of American films I had downed from earliest youth. But my instant recognition that 'D' landing in Stafford was located in the gaol was the best possible confirmation for my companion's belief that he had seen me there.

"You have one on me," he urged delightedly, coming close and putting an arm around my shoulder just as Alf returned and at once took the order. "I like the golden wave in your hair," whispered my new friend softly, gently stroking my hair and squeezing my hand, his fingers intimate in my palm. The juke-box was playing "Midnight in Moscow". I could smell the sweetness of his hair. I hoped Alf, and any others, were not looking.

A dual vision of Uncle Milton Barraclough's freezing face and the works' safe, one as hard as the other, came to disturb me, but the lager, the music and the man hugging me were far more over-powering, and Uncle Milton's grim spectre was quickly exorcised. I lingeringly returned the pressure of my new friend's hand.

"Let's take our drinks into the singing-room," he said. "There's more life in there. This yours?"

He picked up my umbrella and with it upheld like a phallus led the way to where the juke-box glittered and throbbed the question 'What kind of man am I, To fall in love like this?' among the blue-jeaned young men gathered around it or grouped noisily at the tables. Evelyn was downing a glass of stout as she stood tray in hand, jagging with her body and smiling at Norman Povis who was leaning on the juke-box.

The only other women in the room were two hefty overpowdered not so young women sitting coyly together as they surveyed the men. They gave me a rather curious look, I thought.

"What's your name?" my new companion asked as we seated ourselves at a table.

"John Anselm."

"I'm Frank Jeffers. You'll have heard of me."

I shook my head in surprise, he sounded so sure I must have heard of him. He brought his face closer to defeat any eaves-droppers, though it seemed unnecessary in the direct noise-shadow of the juke-box. I saw he had freckles. His hand under the table roved over my leg as he murmured, "I'd stay with you tonight, only I've a job on. You can't trust this lot here much. Alf Shaw's all right, though."

I did not find anything to say to this whispered confidence as I was still wondering whether to declare I had never been on 'D' landing, and as I was in any case so taken up with looking at him and revelling in his presence. He had a bold boyish way—such utter confidence in all he did—and a fine manly voice. I could sense the muscles under his clothes.

"Come on, Johnny boy. Drink it up. What about a strong instead of that bottled water? Try a strong," he urged me, and like a lamb I followed, switching to strong ales after all those lagers.

The pop songs become more hypnotically loud, Frank more beautiful and all else oblivion. I remember him telling me he had been that day to a funeral (of all things). "I'd dug the grave," he explained. "Part-time you know. I'm just waiting till I get my licence back." Somehow I gathered that he had driven a lorry. I remember, too, my being introduced as "a mate of mine—Johnny" to at least one of the blue-jeaned company, probably more than one. What I said or how I behaved I do not remember.

Then the lights were plunged on and off. There were roars from Alf. My glass vanished. I was in the night-air with Frank. The yellowy clock on the Co-op tower showed eleven and a crescent moon was sailing over the Hawkward factory chimneys.

He had an arm about me and I was clinging to him. We wove in the darkness tinder the tall sycamores—he breaking from me as the headlights of cars picked us out or whenever he hissed "Here's a rozzer" and a caped, silhouetted policeman would pass by to Frank's polite "Good-night constable."

I do not remember much more; only the crescent moon sharp and high above the trees and his eyes big and bright as he embraced and kissed me against a sycamore.

He produced a comb to readjust his hair which I had been ruffling. "I'll do you tomorrow night," he said. "I'll wait for you in the Whistle."

I must have been able to wamble the rest of the way with the aid of my umbrella, for I remember noticing that Miss Bee's light was still on and her hydrangea looked wet in the moonlight. I hope I did not drop my shoes too loud.

CHAPTER TWO

I awoke to the telephone's ringing and, from a glance at the alarm-clock which I could not have set to go off last night, the fainting knowledge that I was an hour late for work. Worse still, it was Milton Barraclough himself on the line, sounding as inclement as outer space.

"What the hell do you think you are playing at, young Anselm? The batch for Italy is going off, or would have done but for you. What are you doing there? How can anyone be late for one o'clock in the day?"

"It's my stomach—I've the most terrible diarrhoea."

"Harumph!" came from Milton in disbelief like a jeer. "When will you be here? Not that you're irreplaceable, it's just the inconvenience. You should have 'phoned. I like my staff to be reliable. You are not reliable."

"My stomach..."

"My arse!" He paused. "Try slippery elm—works wonders. And bread and cheese. I want you here for three, and you can stay later." He put the 'phone down.

I had never been late for work before; I had always been terrified of Uncle Milton. Feeling annihilated I sat naked under the shock of taking him like this on my opening consciousness. It was a while before I was steady enough to find some aspirins and put the kettle on. In between my agitation over Uncle Milton I began to recall in bits what I had been doing last night. Being kissed by a man all up Bradford Road! I could just imagine what Uncle Milton thought of homosexuality and what he would think of me. He had not thought much before.

9

I felt utterly aghast at myself. Yet I could not repress a small pride at my prompt excuse; it must have taken Milton in a bit or be would not have recommended slippery elm, whatever that was. Moreover as I thought of Frank I felt less worm-like and outlawed in my own esteem. It was so beautiful and sacred—the word 'sacred' came to me as the right one—to be touched intimately by a lover. It was my first true communion with a fellow-being. No, I would not be ashamed. I would never regret it.

Only, I wished I had set the alarm-clock properly.

After five years at Barraclough's I no longer had any interest in my work. Had there been any reasonable choice I would not have gone there in the first place. I was interested in languages and literature and people; chick-rearing and mathematics were not among my enthusiasms. But Barraclough was my father's first cousin. It had been the goal of my parents' ambition that I should one day enter Barraclough's and, with Milton's prompting, work my way up to a directorship. Barraclough's put a gloom on my childhood—there was the inevitability of the condemned cell in my future. Uncle Milton looked in those days just as he did now. We used to dine with him every year, on Boxing Day, and he would ask me arithmetic questions. He used to give expensive presents, I admit, but they were of a useful nature; my preference was for the purely ornamental—the sort of things which no decent boy is expected to like and which I never dared to say I wanted. In the school-stories which I used to read, lying on the parlour floor, my sympathies were always with the non-English caddish types who betted, wore rings and smoked scented cigarettes, just as in historical romances I enjoyed reading of the heroes who wore powder-blue satin frogged with silver. Uncle Milton and my grandmother Barraclough (whom I remembered as always wearing an outsize tortoise-shell and mother-of-pearl hair comb which I envied) did not approve of women who wore slacks and were both given to using the word 'frippery' about those items of female adornment of which they disapproved. They were unlikely to have approved of them on a male.

My father was a much more likeable and easy character than his cousin, but he had not been so successful in life and he admired and deferred to Milton in every way. I did not want to let my father down and I had enough sense to appreciate that to earn one's daily bread must in most cases be uncongenial. Nor was Barraclough's in actuality too bad.

I think it was Milton who suggested to my parents that I ought to live nearer to the hatchery, though I had asserted my independence of him by not living right on the hatchery doorstep. At the flat I was not too far away, but I was far enough to feel my brief free time disassociated from my working life. As a family connection and potential director, my time was the firm's in Milton's eyes, and for the last year I had worked to a time-table of his devising, by which I would often work through the night and then return to work some time the same day. Milton required very little sleep himself and assumed others were the same. Work at Barraclough's had become unspeakably dreary, with the added strain of my sustaining the role of a sedate young accountant. Other young men had wives and children as an emotional balance, but I could have neither. Unless, indeed, in Frank I found a new centre of being, one who would make ambition worthwhile. He was hardly out of my thoughts all that afternoon and evening.

I did not reach the Pole and Whistle till a quarter past ten. The bar was jammed with labourers and the singing-room was packed, the juke-box roaring. Frank was nowhere to be seen. Evelyn served me with a drink. I stood rather dazed and depressed with an argument about the rates of pay for dyers' labourers at two different firms going on around me.

An elderly labourer with a placid happy face addressed me unexpectedly. "What would you say is the heavier—a pound bag of feathers or a pound bag of iron? Don't rush to answer. You're right. I can see you're an intellectual."

"Frank Jeffers left a message for you," said Alf, seeing me. "He's had to leave but he'll be back before closing time, so will you wait for him."

"You're a friend of Frank's?" asked the placid labourer.

"Yes."

"He's a funny chap. Did you hear he's been digging graves at Nasebottom, Alf?"

"He'll never be happy till he has his licence back," replied Alf rather oddly.

"He drove the hearse for Herbert Bryan's funeral."

"He'll catch it if he's copped," Alf declared.

"I wouldn't want him around at my funeral," said someone, "snitching the handles off the coffin."

"Don't worry, they'll bury you in lime, mate," someone else put in.

There was a crash from the games-room and a high-pitched scream followed by a noise like the trundling of a barrel. A man was blubbering hysterically. Alf moved with portly speed. "Gentlemen, have a thought for me," he implored as two flying and rolling bodies crashed out of the games-room, past him into the gents, where someone considerately held the door open. There was a rush of young men from the singing-room into the corridor to watch the fight. Someone at the front excitedly bawled a description of the battle to those at the back.

"We'll just have to bar cards if they carry on like this," said Evelyn in the half-emptied bar-room. "I was all morning doing that lavatory. Blood takes some washing out."

"Heenan has been asking for trouble all night," said an apologist. "He was warned he'd get it in the mush if he cheated a third time."

Heenan, if he was the one, was making enough din for a thousand murder victims, with shrieks and sobs in a very high key. The voice from the front informed us that Heenan's head was being thrust down the pot.

No one, I noticed, even mentioned calling the police.

"What the hell's going on?" asked Frank, appearing at the back of the crowd as the door rubber-thudded behind him. He was no longer in the black clothes of last night, but in velvety brown corduroys and a thick yellow sweater. Right at once he found his way to the thick of the fight and (feeling annoyed at his interference) I heard his voice raised in command, supplication and threat. The crowd ebbed back. A large fat young labourer, breathing in loud snorts, appeared with another large fat young labourer whose mouth was blooded, eye closed and hair dripping. They were pumping each other's hands in profuse good-will and comradeship like a pair of heads of state, with Frank clapping them on the back; while some anonymous benefactor bought us all drinks. As I looked at Heenan, whose face was growing more discoloured and bloated as he dabbed at the blood with a dirty rag, I thought "what babies, what cruel little boys these grown Englishmen are!" But Frank pinched my bottom and I stopped philosophising. We went into the singing-room that was packed; there were a few young females in tonight and a clear space before the 'Ladies' was being used as a dance floor for the twist. A young sailor was loudly drunk at a corner table, and there was a batch of young lads who could not have been of an age to drink. I explained to Frank why I had arrived late.

"The night's young yet," he said tolerantly. "Hey, Derek! What about going on to your Madge's after?"

Derek was a merry-faced young man in a good suit; by day he was a plasterer. It was already closing time at the 'Whistle' and Frank's suggestion was widely welcomed. By eleven o'clock, half-an-hour after the official closing time, when the 'Whistle' was just making a move to drink up with the juke-box still throbbing for the last determined dancers, about twelve of us piled into two small vans outside and set off over the hills to the inn managed by Derek's sister and brother-in-law. I sat on Frank's knees. There were shouts and protests all the way from the others bumping and suffocating in the narrow space, and jeers at the other van whenever it caught up with us. The road cut right through the moors with cat's eyes set all along the way. Under the crescent moon high among the racing clouds we saw a sign 'The Three Virgins' and screeched into a large courtyard where a couple of cars stood before the small inn. The lights were still on but we did not enter by the front door, where a board declared 'Coaches Welcome'. Past a dolley-tub, some outhouses and a yard with toilets, we stumbled and came blinking into the pub by the back door. Derek immediately entered into a lively argument with his sister, who was standing on the stairs with her hair in curlers and who insisted that she had to be up in time for the coaches in the morning. The brother-in-law and a barman were still washing and tidying up after the last night's drinkers. A group of well-dressed people who were still drinking looked startled as we came in.

"Well, say you're residents if anybody comes, that's all I've got to say," said Derek's sister, "except that I'll tell mam when I see her that you're boozing too much, young Derek. You know where it got you last time. And I've got to get up for those coaches. Some of us work."

Frank and Derek decided that there should be a kitty and, with groans from some, ten shillings was subscribed by everyone present. We were ranged mainly around the stone brass-hung fireplace where logs were burning. A long fair youth stretched himself out on the fleecy hearth-rug. He dashed off a few chords on a guitar and was about to give us music.

"You can cut that guitar out," called Derek's sister, reappearing at the top of the stairs, "for a start."

The landlord winked at us, and between serving us with drinks, he and the barman stolidly worked on, upturning all the chairs except those used by the other party and ours.

Only the drivers of the vans were not drinking beer, but apart from Derek, no one seemed any the worse for the beer and the heat. There was much talk but, as is usual with conversation among drinkers, it was less the substance than the way in which things were said that was interesting. I said nothing at all, content with what seemed my life-long role of listener and looker-on. Besides, it seemed to me that nothing I had lived or liked would interest the present company, neither the hatchery business nor classical music would provide a suitable subject. I was daunted by the experience and freedom of these young men in their bright shirts and fancy shoes—

they had no sexual inhibitions whatever; they seemed to have large sums of money to spend and no responsibility in their jobs, and they were very well informed on jazz-music, cars and maintenance. Most of them seemed to have been already married and separated; I had not before appreciated how largely the avoidance of paying court-orders enters into the lives of young men. Amid all this Frank was the acknowledged expert, consulted and deferred to on points of law. Now and then he would throw me an intimate glance and smile, and stop paying attention to the company so that we were enclosed in a sphere of our own, till someone would interrupt with, "I say, Frank, do you...?"

But by half-past two the conversation was drying up and the drinks running out. There was a conference about whether to take Derek home to his mother in his present condition or to leave him at The Three Virgins. By now he was reeling and noisy, and wanting to wake his sister up to tell her off for insulting his friends. He was quietly muffled and taken out to one of the vans.

"After we leave you I'll get out at the end of Bradford Road," said Frank quietly to me, "and I'll walk back, so wait for me. The less the others see the better."

The other party had gone. When we were near the vans a count revealed that we were still a few of our number short. A search party was sent back in.

"Well, gents," said the landlord of The Three Virgins as the lost members were rounded up from the toilets, "I don't want you to feel unwelcome, but I'll admit I won't be right downhearted when I've seen the last of you."

It had gone three o'clock in the morning when I approached the flat. In the shaft of light from her sitting-room window I could see Miss Bee outside in a nightdress trimming the hydrangea. I waited in the darkness under the trees for Frank to come up the road. I did not want him to encounter Miss Bee and I only wished my elderly neighbour in the ground-floor flat would keep more orthodox hours. I hardly heard Frank approach—he had a gliding tiger-tread that was almost noiseless—and to my relief Miss Bee whisked indoors just as he came up.

"What's that skirt doing out in her nightie?" he asked.

"Ssh," I whispered. "She's gardening. Her hydrangea." I guided him to the stairs that led to my flat. Fortunately I had a separate entrance; this did secure me some privacy from Miss Bee, who was, however, usually on the watch and ready to pounce whenever I appeared.

I turned on the lights and closed the door. At last, we were alone together.

Frank was surprised by the interior of the flat, as if he had not expected it to be furnished with bookcases, paintings and a piano, or to look so well-kept and cosy. He said he was not in need of a meal but wanted to get to bed straight away. We slipped naked between the sheets and he turned out the light.

His body was so young and beautiful and strong. The sculpture of firm flesh under my hands was a wonder and ecstasy. He hooked his arms over my shoulders and in the manner of sailors made love to me. It was at this time that he told me he had been five years in the marines.

I do not know what time it was when at length, feeling satisfied and wonderfully light and serene, we fell asleep in each other's arms.

In pale darkness I awoke, feeling utterly at peace. Frank lay smiling, his eyes shining. Neither of us stirred. I drank in his presence. The wonderful peace still possessed me. Outside the birds began singing.

At length we made the effort and arose. He was full of high spirits. While I made the breakfast he tried out some of my records on the gramophone. I hoped the sound of 'The Soldiers Chorus' from *The Decembrists* would not reach Miss Bee's extra-sensitive ears.

He sighed luxuriously after breakfast. I urged another cup of tea on him, liking to fuss over him. He had asked for cotton and thread to sew a button on his jacket but, as it was obvious he had never properly sewn on a button before, I did this. He strayed over to the piano and began to play.

16

"Where did you learn to play?" I asked. He did not play well.

"In prison."

"What were you in prison for?"

He did not turn his head but stopped playing. "I killed a woman."

My heart seemed to skid. I sat shocked. He came over and sat on the rug beside me before the electric fire.

"It was an accident. I was driving and had no insurance. It wasn't my car. She walked right into the road, but I'd got a record. Listen, Johnny," he said, grasping me and speaking earnestly, "I'm no good. You shouldn't have anything to do with me. My family don't. I'm the black sheep. I've no licence now and I can't have a job with lorries. That's why I've been part-time digging graves. You've no idea what it's like trying to get work with a record like mine. I shouldn't have come with you, but I don't go with women and I wanted you, Johnny."

"Would you blackmail me?" I asked. "That's worse than murder. If you did try it on me I would go straight to the police, no matter what harm it brought on me."

He was genuinely shocked. My confidence in him came flowing back.

"I've been a swine," he said, "but I've never got so low as blackmail. They've all been little things I've done, except the manslaughter. Didn't you know about me? It was in the Hawkward Advertiser."

"How could I? You were so nice-looking and well-spoken. It's such a waste of your life. You're not doing anything criminal now, are you? How could you be so stupid?"

"I'll be all right when I get my licence back. It's only another ten months. Everybody dropped me like a hot cake after I'd been in the first time."

I was upset for him and bemused. "You're still young. You don't want all your life ruined."

He laughed. "You're a proper little worrier. But you're right. I don't want to go back to prison. I remember when they closed the

17

cell-door on me for the first time." His face saddened. I snapped the thread of cotton and handed him back his jacket.

"I hope the way's clear," he said, gazing out of the window. Miss Bee was usually outside with the first light, setting titbits for our local squirrel and strewing porridge-oats for the birds. "Will you be in The Whistle tonight? That's where you can usually reckon on finding me. It's my second home, so to speak. Alf doesn't mind me running up a bit of a bill."

"I'll be there," I said. "But you will try not to get into trouble again, Frank?"

"They'll not keep me in stir again," he said, doing his hair before a mirror. "And, Johnny, you keep your mouth shut about us. You look respectable but how am I to know?"

Before I could hotly reply to this, he was at the front door surveying the road to make sure his departure was unobserved. With a smile he patted my cheek, and silent-footed as an Indian rapidly descended the steps.

I watched his figure disappear into the trees. He had a very slinky mocassined movement—like a cat-burglar. The thought struck home that burglary was probably among his offences. I sat by the electric fire for a while amid the riot of conflicting emotions. I felt a serenity and peaceful sense of fulfilment from our night together, but worry and alarm at the discovery that he had been so implicated in crime. I knew that I would be loyal to him though it brought me to destruction, for to love him and be loved by him was infinitely more precious than a life without.

It was with a strong sense of foreboding and yet with a new central peace that I eventually set off for work.

CHAPTER THREE

During the next few weeks I found myself being greeted in the streets by numerous young men whose faces and names I could not identify until a dredging of the memory hauled them up as patrons of The Pole and Whistle. I had believed I had a good visual memory, but the beer I drank with Frank as well as the heat and noise of the pub made it difficult to retain all the numerous shifting faces of the pub's population. It was with a start, therefore, that in the cold clear day I would encounter a beaming face that had last been nocturnally drifting in the singing-room. The greetings, which would come unexpectedly from among a gang mending a hole in the road or from the cab of a passing lorry, would be of great warmth. As a friend of Frank's I was 'in', and I was further guaranteed by the Christian name footing which I was on with Alf and Evelyn. I was now a 'regular' of the Whistle and admitted to the select company which stayed drinking in the bar till midnight or later, once the masses had been excluded. Indeed, I was more regular than the regulars for I never drank anywhere else, but with the purpose of meeting Frank, spread wings for the Whistle like a homing pigeon whenever I had finished at Barraclough's.

It was seldom that Frank was not at the Whistle, though how he could afford to be always there on unemployment pay I supposed must be a tribute to his unofficial skill with cards rather than part-time grave-digging. On two occasions he was absent from the Whistle and when he came tapping at the flat in the small hours he explained that he had been keeping his mother company before the television and come out the back way once she was safely in bed.

From Alf, in a confidential mood, I gathered that Mrs. Jeffers was convinced Frank was an innocent boy whom everyone, especially the police, maligned or led astray. She had acted up to this belief by once dramatically appearing in the Whistle and telling a company of labourers in the games-room that she had seen a deterioration in Frank's character since he had met the abandoned lot of them.

"Mums usually make a fuss of the youngest," said Alf. "Personally, I was an orphan. Hence the self-reliance," he added with a wink.

"And I don't think," said Evelyn crossly. She was wearing a turban, as in the attempt to go a fashionable rust-red at the house of a hairdressing friend, something had gone wrong and her hair had come out green. "What did you marry for, if you're so self-reliant? You or any other man?" The mishap to the hair had not improved her temper and Alf, who had been publicly snubbed several times, received much sympathy in his absence from the customers. "Pity it didn't turn her bald," was all the sympathy Evelyn had from the games-room. "Norman Povis wouldn't have cared for that," someone slyly observed.

I was not particularly perturbed at learning that Frank lived with an observant and protective mother. I just looked on it as an obstacle to his coming to live openly and permanently with me at the flat. What plucked at my heartstrings with disturbing sadness amid the trance-like allegro of this opening new relationship was the thought of my own mother.

The first Sunday after I met Frank I was working and so could not meet him, but on the second Sunday I was free. I had always gone to my parents for Sunday dinner when I was not working. My mother looked forward to seeing me. I rang her up to tell her I would not be coming. I had never lied to her in my life, and now as I made some glib excuse about having work to do for the firm, and heard her rather worried but utterly believing and trusting voice at the other end of the line, a tight feeling of self-contempt so depressed and weighed on me that only by effort could I prevent this unease and anguish from being detected in my voice. I had shared so much with my mother and sister that the awareness I could never mention the love of my adult life to them made me desolate and self-sick. They were the only people I would not want to deceive and, indeed, I knew that with their intimate knowledge of me it would be difficult ever to do so. I was glad to postpone the day when I would have to act in the family circle as if nothing wonderful had ever happened to me. I spent the whole of that Sunday with Frank.

It was around this time that after a meeting of the directors, Milton called the leading members of the staff together and announced that the firm was shortly to have the services of an electronic brain. Sara would be no commonplace aid in the computation of accounts. She was to function on a massive scale in the statistical analysis of breeding records and genetic data so that Barraclough's would be able to offer improved poultry stock years ahead of rival firms. The electronic computer, Milton informed us, would cost fifty thousand pounds and would mean a rearrangement and shake-up of the whole firm. The old manual methods of record-keeping would be dispensed with.

Milton was quite hoarse with explaining to shareholders and reporters the many implications of his firm's being the first in the field with a computer in Britain. Rapt in my private happiness I was glad not to have him on my back all the time. I sleep-walked through quantities of work of which I had not the least recollection. Really, the introduction of the computer was like an earthquake in the firm's hitherto old-fashioned family methods of business. To back modern science to the extent of fifty thousand pounds indicated a colossal war of faith within Milton. But I slept through it all. At the staff meeting I had heard him as from afar saying that it needed all hands to the pumps and the firm could carry no passengers in the strenuous days ahead.

But I no longer truly cared about being passenger or crew on the big electronic Barraclough line. I preferred a coracle with Frank on the open sea, and drifted all the time further from my family and work.

CHAPTER FOUR

Lying cradled in bed with Frank as the light of dawn came into the room I would be speechless with happiness. He, on the contrary, was more communicative and chatty at this time than at any other, and with his arm about me and his young laughing face tilted upwards as if sculptured on a tomb, would tell me of the more hilarious aspects of life in the marines, or how he wangled his way into becoming a trustee in charge of towels for the prison baths. I loved these early morning confidences when he was in a restful good humour and revealed so much of himself, and he also, I considered, looked his most beautiful with the morning light on his exposed throat and shoulders. We were in this early morning bliss when he mentioned that he had considered starting up as a window-cleaner.

"Neil Crossley wants a partner," said Frank. "If I put up twenty pounds I can buy myself in, and I reckon I'd get it back quickly enough from the profits of two of us working."

"I could let you have twenty pounds," I said, "if that's all that is stopping you."

"Oh, I can get the loan of twenty nicker from Les Barron easily enough," said Frank carelessly. "I don't want to start taking money from you, honey, else I won't know when to stop. You sit on your dough, I warn you. No, I don't know whether it's worth twenty pounds—though that would give me a half-share in the ladders and cart. I think I'll give it a try; it'll help out my dole money, anyway."

"Your dole?" I exclaimed. "But if you're working as a window-cleaner..."

"I need the dole for drink money," Frank explained patiently. "I don't *live* on it, my darling."

We listened to the birds' singing and I eyed Frank's tattoo for the thousandth time.

"And another thing," said Frank contemplatingly, "I don't know how far I can trust Neil. I sometimes get the idea that he's a bit of a dishonest bugger."

I was checking figures at work with Miss Anderson of the Wages' Department when, happening to look up, I was stupefied to see Frank floating like a golliwog at the window. My brisk working manner left me; I lost control of the figures and just stared as Frank gave me a coarse wink and leered with his lips pouted in a kiss. Miss Anderson took this as a tribute to her femininity.

"Really, English working men," she said, not ill-pleased, as Frank made a massaging movement with his chamois leather. I noticed that he had bicycle-clips around his trousers and that his blue open-neck shirt particularly suited him, and I had deduced he must be standing on a ladder to appear thus outside a third-floor window, before I made an implausible excuse to Miss Anderson and hastily left the Wages' Department. Frank could hardly expect me to blow him kisses, not with Milton Barraclough as a possible spectator.

Half-an-hour later I ventured out again with some papers for Dr. Smith, the Chief Statistician, but at the turn in the stairs I could see Frank outside another window, soundlessly whistling, and there was Milton coming up the stairs on the way to Dr. Smith and the fabulous Sara. I darted into a nearby toilet, where there was a wrinkled frosted glass, and with a beating heart leant there wondering how long I could safely remain before search parties began hunting for me. I couldn't keep dodging about the place all day; the works might not be a modern building but there had been no stinting of glass in its construction. I had never been so conscious of the number of windows in my place of employment.

After a while I became calm again and no longer knew why I had been agitated. The thing to do, I told myself, was to carry on as usual and just ignore Frank if he appeared. And if he should show up at a window while I was alone in the room I could ask him to behave more discreetly. I returned to Miss Anderson and resumed our checking.

The cleaners must have moved to the windows on the other side of the building for I saw no more of them and had I forgotten they were about when later in the afternoon, as Mr. Sutcliffe was with me, I heard the flip-flop and squeak of a chamois-leather at the window. I was careful not to look in the direction of the sound, but sideways in the chromium vase on the desk I saw Frank mirrored. At last Mr. Sutcliffe went and I turned to the window. I hoped no one would come for a moment. Frank pressed his nose on the glass and beckoned me eagerly over to him.

"You big galoot," I said angrily, "making it so obvious to everyone!" He put his tongue out and slanted his eyes so that I had to laugh, and he tapped the glass to make me understand that he couldn't hear me and wanted me to open the window. I shook my head in refusal, and he promptly produced a glass-cutter from a pocket and made as if he would use it. I was alarmed at this and tried to shoo him off, but as he couldn't hear me I thought I would have to open the window to tell him to buzz off.

The windows at Barraclough's opened inwards and to reach them you needed a hooked pole both for the small top part and for the large main window which was hinged at the middle. I was never very adept with the window-pole at the best of times.

"You'll get us both in disgrace," I hissed at Frank as soon as I succeeded, fearful that at any moment someone might come in.

"Oh go on. There's no one here. Aren't you going to offer me a cup of tea?

"You'll break the window if you lean like that."

"My water's dirty anyway. A window-cleaner always stops for a chat with a pretty young piece."

"No, Frank, you can't come in these windows," I said firmly. "They won't...There!"

"I've cut my bloody leg. Probably an artery."

I attempted to help him, fearing that he would go crashing backwards to the ground below, but with the window swinging awkwardly the only result of my help was that he put a hand through another large pane and was trampling about in the glass like a fly in a tray of clear toffee. The next instant they were all about us too. Mr. Sutcliffe, Mr. Greenwood, angry elderly faces. It was as if the entire staff of the hatchery had been summoned by the noise, and here too was Milton Barraclough, with bloodless lips and the voice of Hitler ordering millions to annihilation

I closed my eyes in horror. In my dizzying, palpitating condition I saw and heard nothing till out of the wobbling cotton-wool of my sensations I heard Frank coolly say, "I don't know who you think you are, mate," and disbelievingly saw he was addressing Milton.

"Who is the ineffable idiot in charge of our outside cleaning?" Milton calmly enquired. "I want to see him in my office at once. As for this drunken semblance of a human being, find out his name and address so we can send him our bill and call the police if he is not off the premises within five minutes. Anselm, I'm addressing you. Get your finger out."

It was the first time Milton had rebuked me in public and it was about the only thing wanting to complete my discomfiture.

"I'll sue the old crab-apple for damage to my trousers," said Frank. "Has anyone got a pin?"

"If I were you, young man," said Mr. Sutcliffe ominously, "I'd get out of here fast and have less to say."

"I've my bucket and ladder to think of, chum," said Frank.

"Do put some T.C.P. on those cuts," said Miss Anderson, the gentle-hearted. "I usually have some on me."

"I wouldn't worry unduly about a bucket," said Mr. Sutcliffe stiffly.

"I'll come down with you, Frank," I said hurriedly. There was a stale smell of malt whenever Frank spoke.

"I'll claim damages if my leg goes septic," he called back as I led him off, his right trouser-leg dangling. "Those windows are mucking death-traps!"

"I could kill you," I said on the stairs. "But you'll do that soon enough if you get drunk while cleaning windows."

"I'm not drunk. I think the mild was off in the Whistle and I had it on an empty stomach."

"You've caused enough mischief here."

There was a cry as we came out and a furious Neil Crossley, who had been working at another side of the building and had just heard of his new partner's mishap, bore indignantly down on us.

"All right, all right, all right," snapped Frank. "So I broke a sixpenny bit of glass. I admit it. There's no need to keep opening your trap."

"I've lost the sub-contracting through you," Neil shouted. "You big ape!"

"If you want to wear that bucket for a hat...."

"He's upset," I told Neil Crossley and stood in front of Frank whose fist all but blacked my eye. "Frank please. Do keep calm. You can settle all these things later." I became inspired. "If the police are brought in it will only come out you were working while on the dole. Why don't you go and have a hot pie and peas at the Transport Cafe, and I can meet you in the Whistle at about seven."

"If that old geezer was my boss," said Frank, departing, "I'd slip some rat poison in his sedlitz powder." At the gate he glanced back at the building where we could see people at the windows watching us. He eyed the rain-pipes. "It'd be the easiest place to do a job."

"No, Frank," I said firmly, and lied. "We never keep money on the premises."

"I don't know what I'm going to do about this," said Frank, fishing a grubby piece of paper from a trouser pocket. It was about two weeks later.

"What?" I asked from the bed.

I looked at the paper he threw me; it was a bill with the Barraclough heading addressed to the firm that had employed Neil Crossley as a sub-contractor on the windows. "It's not made out to you," I commented.

"No, Neil gave it me. They gave it him. He never stops bloody-well moaning I lost him the contract. Well, I've got more on my plate

26

than that little lot. A new pair of pants come before fixing your bloody windows."

"Which you broke," I reminded him icily, thinking of all the tirades I had to hear from Milton as if I personally engaged the window-cleaners, not to mention the draughts that had blown in about the temporary cardboard before the panes were restored.

"I don't suppose you want a gas-geyser?" Frank added hopefully, drawing on his socks.

"Where did you get it?"

"Not where you think. Where would I nick a gas-geyser?"

"You'd manage anything if you were drunk."

"Well, know-all, it happens to come from my mam's and I bought it—strictly legal. It's a good one. There's room for it by your sink. I'd install it for you."

"No thanks."

"That's all my assets, Johnny boy. Anyway they may forget about the bill. It's not my pigeon in any case; they can't touch me when the bill isn't made out to me."

"We don't want any trouble," I said, knowing Milton never forgot anything. "Do stop clattering about, Frank, Miss Bee will start complaining."

"You're always scared," said Frank, springing on to the bed and using it as a trampoline. "Boy, have they got you tamed!"

Nevertheless, I settled the bill.

CHAPTER FIVE

Looking at night through the back window of the flat, I could see a pin-point brightness in the dark valley to the north of Hawkward, and I knew then that my parents had left on the outside light fixed to the gate of their house. For weeks I had put off actually encountering my family, though I had spoken to my mother by telephone. I knew she was becoming anxious at my continued absences on Sundays. I knew I would have to meet her sooner or later. On the Sunday when Frank had to accompany his mother for a stay of some days with her relations in a seaside town, I gathered myself together for the encounter.

I had become an entirely different person. I knew my mother would recognise the change in me, and I dreaded her probing the reason for my new and unmistakeable radiance. There was the same alteration in me as there would have been in a daughter who had found fulfilment in love. It would be impossible to disguise my overflowing inner gladness. My father was unlikely to notice anything; about my sister I was not sure. Changes had crept into my dress and appearance since I had met Frank, so now I took care to remove the betraying brightness in my attire and studied to be as sober and masculine as possible for this visit to my parents.

As I came up to the house the dogs ran out barking and after them came my mother, holding a walking-stick and prepared either to chase the goats away or challenge a trespasser. The villagers of Draft were given to entering the woods by the side of my parents' house, though there was in fact no right of way on that path. Seeing me she became sunny.

My mother was settling into the comfort of the fifties and there was a cosy matronliness now to her appearance that I found attractive. I had schooled myself to utter calm so that I should be at my ease and give her no cause for alarm.

"You do look well, John," she said. She gazed at me puzzled. "Somehow you look different."

I wondered what I had not attended to in my appearance, the betraying womanlinesses in the way I wore my clothes or combed my hair. Or there may have been something in my manner, a manifestation of my nature now polarised to Frank's maleness. But patting the delighted dogs I allowed myself to be escorted around the garden to view the plants which had come to glory in my absence. I had presented mother with the seeds of the oriental poppies that, with their shades of flame, added a fine blaze to the old gardens. But every so often would be too plain evidence of a mouthful of plant filched by a goat, and it seemed tactful to gloss over these.

"Your father," said my mother as if thought reading, "just will not stake out those goats—especially that young one who is a devil. She has ruined the roses of Sharon, and they were doing so well."

My father, I knew, would be inside before the television.

"Is Jessie at home?" I enquired.

"She's gone up to get the Sunday papers. The boy leaves them at Mrs. Booth's now. It's a wonder you didn't see her as you came down. She shouldn't be long."

"I came the other way."

"There she is now."

I watched the white flash of my sister's dress appearing and re-appearing through the trees as she came down the path to the house. Jessie was a year younger than I was. She was secretary to a firm in Pilney and travelled there every week-day by bus from Draft. Occasionally her firm did some haulage work for us and I would then have a chat with her by telephone, but we had had no work done for us by her firm for several months.

She came tripping down to us, smiling, calm and unflustered. Jessie always had an unruffled sweetness. The sun lit her fair uncovered arms and flashed a diamond and sapphire ring she was wearing. I wondered whether it betokened an engagement or was for ornament, but I could not remember which was the engagement finger. She told us that she had been in to see Mrs. Booth's new-born grandchild, "a lovely baby boy," and amid the enthusiasm for our old neighbour's first grandchild I forgot to ask about the ring.

My father greeted me in his sweet absent manner and fell on the Sunday papers, from which he emerged only to make an enquiry about the joint.

As Sara, the electronic computer, had been much in the news I had to give a personal account of it to Jessie and my mother, mixed with a complaint about the awkward hours the re-organisation of the firm meant for me. My mother made a reference to Uncle Milton and for a moment my heart sank, but he could not have been making any complaints and we passed from him to more cheerful topics. Jessie and my mother were to go to Scotland for a holiday; an old school friend of Jessie's was working her way around the world and had written some interesting letters; the family were thinking of acquiring an Alsatian pup to scare trespassers; the piano on which I first learnt to play had been re-tuned.

The sun was strong in what had been the living-room of the converted farm house and as we sat at table and Jessie was speaking of the route they would follow, all was so normal, cheerful and untroubled that I felt a stab of anguished awareness at the misery I would bring into this room should my relationship with Frank be divulged. How would my mother and Jessie look at me then, or endure the contempt and aversion of the small community around which scandal was so merciless? I drove off the thought so that my gloom might not be evident.

"More meringue?" asked my mother, who knew I enjoyed Jessie's cooking. She was facing the window; knife in hand she cried indignantly, "The cheek of it! With two dogs not on a lead and no right of way!"

I caught a glimpse of a youth in a bright shirt as he crossed the side of the house.

"Now, dear," said my father. "No use making a fuss."

"They've knocked the wall down several times with their climbing over," Jessie explained. "Nothing stops them."

"And your father says it's no use making a fuss!" exclaimed my mother, sitting down to recover from her indignation. She had coloured so violently that I feared she might burst an artery.

"It's not worth risking your health over," I soothed. "It looks as if it's something you'll have to live with."

"Never!" said my mother. "They break the wall down and have their dogs trampling my garden just because they're too lazy to walk round the proper way. Your father should assert himself."

"I don't see what harm they're doing," said my father. "Most of the time," he hastily added.

My mother sighed. "They're gone too quickly for a policeman to get here in time to catch them. And they're so rude."

"I wouldn't try to catch them myself, mother; you might get harmed. Can't you see the solicitors again and see what legal remedies there are?" I thought of some of the youths who frequented The Pole and Whistle and was uneasy at the thought of any elderly woman trying to stop them trespassing. "There are some pretty nasty customers about today. They wouldn't hesitate to use violence on someone weaker."

"It isn't right, John," said my mother, not in the least convinced and not in the least frightened by my talk into being discreet. "There's no right of way here and I won't be terrorised, whoever they are. One can't just give in to wrong."

CHAPTER SIX

On the Friday night I arrived at The Pole and Whistle where Frank was waiting for me at the bar. He was wearing a new pearl-grey suit about which I at once asked a question and learnt that his relations had bought it for him. His face was a delightful pink-brown that made his teeth whiter. He looked more handsome and elegant than ever.

"God! I could have done with you," he swore softly for my ears alone and squeezed me less secretly. "Lying on the beach and only able to look. I wish we could go somewhere together for a holiday. I've had nothing but old hens around me for a week. Are you coming to the dance tonight?"

"What dance?"

"Why, the Farmers' Ball, of course."

"But you're not a farmer—And I don't dance much."

"You don't have to be a farmer to go to a Farmers' Ball," said Frank, impatient at my ignorance. "I'll show you how to dance. You'll be all right with me."

"Have you got tickets then?"

"Tickets?" He looked offended. "You just leave it to me."

"I'm not washed," I protested.

"You can get a wash at our house. It doesn't liven up till later so we'll have a few hours here first. Are you going to the dance, Evelyn?"

"You bet," Evelyn announced. She had had her hair dyed especially and wore large copper discs in her ears; she was in a skin-tight green dress which made her look Minoan. There was an eager unrest about her. I envied her sharp perfume and powder-laden air.

"Alf going?" enquired Frank.

"That old misery?" said Evelyn looking cat-like with disgust, and hissed to the crowded bar, "I don't know why I ever married such a selfish pig. What life is it for a woman serving you lot? I'm going to the Farmers' Ball, I told him, if I have to die or get divorced. What do you think of my ear-rings, John?"

"They go with the dress," I said cautiously.

"I've got a tea-pot stand at home that matches 'em," said Bill Pratt who farmed in the hills outside Hawkward. "Just the same size."

"Ha, ha," said Evelyn.

"I think John would look better with them," Les Barron called from the singing-room where the juke-box for once was not on.

"He hasn't got his ears pierced," said Evelyn.

"Not yet," said Les in a dry sort of way.

"Have a brandy on me," Bill Pratt offered Evelyn, as if to placate her for the jest about her ear-rings.

"Thanks, I will. I know you can afford it with the price you ask for eggs. I could just," declared Evelyn, holding a glass under and squirting herself a generous allowance of brandy, "get stinking tight tonight."

Alf came in, stern-lipped, his eyes puffy. "Go easy with the brandy there," he cautioned.

"Oh you mean sod," responded Evelyn. "Bill Pratt's bought it me."

It was not the first time service at the bar had been attended by a matrimonial Punch and Judy; sparring of some sort was usually in progress. But tonight there was a quality of strength in Evelyn's defiance, a silencing surliness and crushed sorrow about the usually gentle Alf. There was a feeling in the air that all hell might break loose. Frank drew me into the games-room. He threw darts aimlessly and refused to be drawn into a game of Black Two. I guessed he would not feel at ease playing in his best suit with the others in their working clothes.

"She's a proper bitch, that Evelyn," he said suddenly. I made no comment "She'll go to the dance with Norman Fovis, you mark my words. Alf won't wear it—she oughtn't to do it when she's got two kids."

"Is there a bar at the dance?" one of the card players in oily blue jeans asked Frank.

"No, the bluebottles opposed it," said Frank. "You know what happened last time." He turned to me. "We'd best cut along to my mam's, then you can have a tea and get washed, and we can come back here to get tanked up. You can't enjoy a dance without some booze."

As we went out of the Whistle, the door closing with its slow rubbery thud, Evelyn at the bar could be heard declaring loudly in her common voice as if she were at an international truce conference, "I'll put the kids to bed, but you can make your own supper…"

In the street Frank spoke out of the side of his mouth as we went along, "My mam will watch us like a hawk but don't you go giving the game away. I've a three-quarter bed so we won't be pushed. I'll try to fix it that you kip with me tonight."

I don't know what I had expected Frank's mother to be like. We had turned into the oldest quarter of Hawkward with its narrow streets and small regularly windowed houses close on top of one another. Old-fashioned gas lamps hung above the entrances to dark alleys where bins stood. It was a bit of England where Jack the Ripper would have blended in well. In a street with stone setts we stopped at the door of a small house with neat net curtains and went in.

"Mam," Frank roared. "I've brought a friend home with me for a bit of tea."

"If he's like the rest of your friends," came the response, "he can go off double-quick. He'll get no tea here."

"If he doesn't," said Frank, "I warn you I'll bop you one, mam."

"Less of that," said the quite unangry voice, "or I'll about you with my washing-stick."

I knew that I must have led a sheltered life as I listened; too astonished for words. Mrs. Jeffers came in from the kitchen, a gentle-looking tiny little woman in her late sixties with silver hair.

"He isn't one of the usual Whistle lot," said Frank, wheedlingly. "He's respectable and educated, mam."

"Then what's he doing with you?" Mrs. Jeffers crisply demanded.

"Oh you're a cheeky monkey!" Frank exclaimed, throwing himself into an arm-chair with one of his legs over the arm. "Now mam, we're going to a dance so look sharp. Open a tin of decent salmon, not that pink muck from Mrs. James!"

"Pink muck from Mrs. James! Listen to Rockerfeller. Oh, this is the Ritz!" Mrs. Jeffers mocked. "And you're not going to any dance. You can do something useful about the house for a change."

"I don't want to flatten you, mam," said Frank good-naturedly.

"A little shrimp like you touch me? That'll be the day!"

"Aye, you're brave behind a washing stick," Frank jeered.

"Get your dirty big leg off that arm," Mrs. Jeffers commanded and her arm came up with something from the side of the dresser. Frank howled in real agony as a long piece of grained wood with a hole in it crashed down smartly on his shin. His eyes ran with tears as he doubled up, nursing his leg.

"I've told you before about sitting properly in that armchair," said Mrs. Jeffers. "Now what would you like, love? Do you fancy a pressed tongue salad?"

"It'll be too much trouble for you," said I, more or less prepared to go. I had never heard a son and mother discourse together like this, and to complete my amazement here was the he-man and tough guy of whom everyone stood in awe at The Pole and Whistle now immobilised in agony under the washing-stick of a frail old lady in her sixties. I regarded with respect the lady who stood to me, as it were, in the relation of mother-in-law.

"Oh, I can see you're a well brought up boy, not like that Tommy Dunkin. If he ever comes here he'll get something as a memento." She poked Frank. "Hang your friend's coat up. What's your name, love? Oh, I like a nice bit of tongue this weather."

When she was in the back-kitchen Frank nudging me whispered, "You're in, Johnny. She likes you. She doesn't take to just anyone, you know."

It was a clean pleasant house with that extra tidiness of dwellings belonging to alert elderly people. In the recesses of the tiled hearth and in a glass cabinet were a number of small glass figures, lovingly collected over the years, and on the walls there hung Dutch figures of bright wood and a wooden plaque with an inscription in Dutch. I learnt that last year Mrs. Jeffers had had a holiday in Holland and these were the trophies, as it were, of the first momentous visit to Europe. Frank looked bored during the recital of the holiday, having heard it all before, but Mrs. Jeffers, encouraged by the first taste, was going to be quite the traveller and, saving up through the working year, was aiming next at Switzerland, I was surprised at the fleeting mention of Mrs. Jeffers working, but it appeared that having worked all her life, her skill in garment making being valued by her employers, she still went to work regularly each day, and this on top of looking after the home and Frank.

Half-an-hour before closing time we returned to The Whistle, Mrs. Jeffers giving Frank a parting piece of advice about not getting into trouble at the dance. "Some of these young girls just lie in wait," said Mrs. Jeffers impressively, "and our Frank's chump enough."

"Now mam," said Frank.

"And if there's a fight you stay out of it," Mrs. Jeffers said. "Keep away from the rough lot. I can see John's a nice respectable boy, so, Frank, if there's any rowdyism come straight home or I'll give you what-for later on."

By the time we left The Whistle (the ten minutes drinking-up time having sped into forty-five) I suspected that the main rowdyism at the dance might be imported by us. Frank's clean shirt was already crumpled and his tie unknotted. It was a hot night anyway, and Frank, in addition, was stoking for the fun of footing it as well as replenishing with Alf in his sorrow. The gentle landlord who had occasional half milds, was gone; instead there was a touchy thing of nerves and jackass laughter, drinking multitudinous gins for rapid oblivion. Evelyn had set off for the dance with Norman Povis and from the way Alf was despairing and disintegrating she had given the impression of meaning never to return. In the end a couple of regulars who lived nearby shut up The Whistle for the night and remained with Alf in the mysterious living-quarters beyond the Ladies, presumably to see him safely to bed.

We by then were at the dance or, rather, at the murky lit entrance to the Gibraltar Ballroom. Here a crowd of young men were hanging around and a policeman, scowling and hot-faced, was moving in front of them.

"You're not getting in without paying, Jeffers," he snarled at Frank as soon as he spotted us.

"You hold your jaw, Hurley," said my hero. "I'm here by invitation."

"Ha, ha," said P.C. Hurley. I put a tight grip on Frank's arm so that he could not be said to have struck the first blow. The lads, hot-breathed with beer, drew in expectantly as Hurley puffed and huffed himself, and I dare say that I who had stepped between Hurley and Frank would have been knocked cold had not someone appeared at the top of the stairs and been greeted by Frank by name as he darted up to meet him. I don't know what occurred between them but in a short while I was being admitted to the dance with Frank to the policeman's vexation. He glowered after us, and my law-abiding soul was disturbed at this my first mild hostile brush with a policeman.

"One in the eye for Hurley," declared Frank triumphantly. "Where's the buffet? I could do with a snack before we dance. Hey—where's the buffet? Thanks, chum."

The buffet was packed with chubby-faced youths and even more numerous girls scrambling for the food. Frank soon emerged from the scrum with a pile of sandwiches for himself and tea and a bun for me. He caught sight of himself in a mirror and still bolting sandwiches whisked me off with him to the gents so that he could tidy himself.

"The tarts will want me to dance with them," he said. "But honestly I don't want to, Johnny. I'd rather dance with you."

I said nothing.

"I don't care what they say. I'll knock the first one down that says owt. You want to dance, don't you?"

"Yes, I want to dance."

"Then let's go."

Inside the swing doors all was in the grip of the loud music sending the chandeliers slowly circling. At one end of the ballroom was the band, then the floor of dancers and at the other end, where we entered, were the non-dancers, groups of those resting from the last dance occupying chairs or standing, while behind them on a tiered platform were those who were here just for the sociable purpose of viewing, or who were too shy or unable to dance. The air was thick with tobacco smoke. Frank kept bobbing away to greet his pals whom he kept spying among the throng. In the meantime my eyes roamed around. I was surprised at the number of young men among the non-dancers on the tiered seats, and even more so at the numerous young women dancing with each other on the dance-floor. A friend of Frank's cracked a joke about this being the Lesbians' ball, but a number of stout matrons encased in tight blue silk dresses and other brightly coloured ones, and red-faced hearty gents made an agricultural nucleus and proved this was a farmers' dance. The music for the dance ended. The number of people on the floor thinned.

"I'm the best fighter of anyone in this room," declared Frank looking around.

New couples were forming. The band started up again with "Midnight in Moscow".

"Come on," said Frank taking my hand, and we took our first steps into the whirling motion of other bodies. I was not a practised or good dancer, though Frank was, but the tune with its sombre catchiness inspired me. Besides, he was so strong and protective and loving that I was given up to him and the music. His fair hair and tanned face were so close, and our bodies fused hand and shoulder moved as one. He brought me utter joy, just as gravely dancing with

38

him in private would have done, but it felt so natural that we should be dancing together that during the dances I forgot anyone could think otherwise. Only momentarily, my gaze went to the other couples passing nearby us; I read the expression on the faces of a youngish man and woman. It was a look not of aversion or disgust, surprise or anger, it was a look of not seeing us. People simply pretended that our bodily images were not there. The toughs, of course, were in awe of Frank; we would scarcely have escaped open comment otherwise. But the nice civilised people ignored us. Perhaps it was a real tolerance on their part. It was the first time I had been excluded by the eyes of my fellow beings and I winced. I might have been one of those reputation-overcast females in Victorian fiction who had turned up at a ball of the local nobility only to be ignored. But it was only for a moment I knew my outcast condition. Frank certainly didn't care a hoot, and in my joy at his close supple presence nothing could overshadow me and I was grateful for a tolerance which could ignore us.

We broke off once for a rest—Frank going to the toilet and scavenging at the now closed buffet—while I sat and surveyed the scene of elderly ladies in bursting dresses, the farmers drowsy at being up so late, the young ones beginning here their romances and married fates. A green sheet of lightning lit up the windows and the lights trembled. The summer storm that had broken outside was not heard through the music and dancing. The dancing was scheduled to end at two but towards one o'clock most of the company had departed. A feeling as if we were the last ghostly survivors of Versailles crept in; with the dancers thinning, there was a pathetic quality to the indomitable gaiety of the band. It was as if life were closing or as if, with our sprightliness now mechanical and unreality in our presences, we would vanish at cock-crow.

"Let's go, Johnny," said Frank. "It's gone a bit dead."

The streets were fresh and wet and a warm drizzle was falling. It was a quarter to two by the yellow-faced Co-op clock.

39

"I said to my mam you might stay—with the dance ending so late —so we'll be all right."

He put his arm around my shoulder, and wordless in our happiness, through the empty streets we returned to his mother's house.

CHAPTER SEVEN

The months of that summer were the happiest of my life. It would have been better if I had been working regular daytime hours and so could have had every evening free. But even as it was, month melted into month unmarred by anxiety. Whenever I had a free evening I would go walking with Frank in the lanes around Hawkward. You could see people and cars approaching a long way off in those lanes and it was only then that he would move his arm from around my waist and wait till they were again out of view. Sometimes if I left work in the late evening when there was a long golden slant on the hills we would stroll to an old abandoned road just outside Hawkward. It was grown over with grass and rabbits played there. Once there was another pair of lovers in our favourite place but we went further on; they were the only ones we ever saw there. We would lie quiet, mindlessly, as the sunlight slipped down the bank, and he would stroke my hair. Sometimes he would produce a bottle of beer from each pocket and it was pleasant to lie on one elbow and drink in the cooling evening. Once—it was after a day when he had been working for a firm of dyers—he fell asleep with his face on my chest. The sun had gone and young stars were trembling through the leaves when he woke. His opened eyes were bright in the dusk. It was as if our twin energies had become one in peace and earth and all space were lapping to infinity with our quiet ecstasy. To the soft breathing of the summer earth we made love under the stars.

As I wandered through the summer lanes with Frank I was surprised at his casual acquaintances with the farms and places we passed. He seemed to have worked everywhere. Sometimes he had worked more than once at the same place, in a different capacity. Between the ages of fifteen and eighteen he must have had a hundred jobs. He had worked on farms; he had installed a lightning conductor on a steeple; he had helped to rig a cable; he had been a coalman. I lost count of the dizzying variety of his fleeting occupations. Even during these summer weeks while still frustrated from having his licence withheld, he was kaleidoscoping from job to job and if I walked out one night with a dyer's labourer the next evening would quite likely find me with a worker in asbestos or a roadman or an ice-cream man. I asked him once if the Labour Exchange didn't find him trying.

"They're bloody useless," he said pungently. "You'd never get a job through them." He added darkly, "They keep the jobs for their favourites. I wouldn't go near 'em."

Sometimes he had schemes or dreams into which I was drawn. There was a cardboard-box factory further south where, according to Frank, one could earn up to twenty pounds a week. We would live snugly together in a caravan, he proposed. He had once, after a tiff with his mother, gone and worked at the cardboard factory, but the loneliness of life in the caravan had got him down. Now he would have me....I had doubts about my prowess with cardboard, but Frank said he could do my work as well as his own—most of the time they just lay about anyway. Or just he would work. I was even more doubtful about being kept. This talk of the cardboard-box factory kept on. Basically I was dubious about Frank's power to stay for more than a few weeks at one job. He had another theme which he introduced from time to time, that we should take to the road together. I was game for this, but the plans for jobs were vague. He made England sound as if it were a well-knit chain of Poles and Whistles stretching from Land's End to the Border like Roman castra, and everywhere chummy fellows would be only too eager to provide us with casual employment. It was an appealing prospect in its way; Frank would have liked to mother me. Only obstinately the image of two hoboes eating lukewarm Scotch broth out of a dusty tin over a feeble roadside fire would arise to make my stomach faintly recoil. It seemed such an arduous roofless, rained-on existence. I would have preferred Australia to do our wandering in, somewhere sunny at least. But Frank had known plenty of people who had been to Australia and said it wasn't all it was cracked up to be; the midges were terrible. And back we would go dreaming to the cardboard-box factory where you could earn up to twenty pounds a week.

We did not linger in the Whistle for Evelyn had not returned since the night of the dance. Alf, left with the two young children, was by turns snappy, over-sensitive, tearful and bad-tempered, and was given to confiding his more intimate woes over the taps. While one sympathised one felt uncomfortable at his misery; landlords must be cheerful and uphold their patrons' precarious satisfaction with themselves and the hour. But here we were trying to inject some brightness into our weepy host. Moreover, one might feel called on to help behind the bar or do some unpaid waiting as the pub was now undermanned and customers could no longer consider themselves a special class. Old stalwarts from among the customers who could be reckoned to know the price of most ales helped in the evenings, but it was amateur good-will. One felt there was something odd and wrong at these familiar faces on the other side of the taps. The pub was no longer stable. Even the beer went off.

A savage anti-feminism revealed itself in the talk. I was surprised at how little popular Evelyn had been. "Her and her ear-rings," was said scornfully, and I heard more than once that Alf hadn't been firm enough—he just hadn't dealt that occasional go-along, which is the true glue of matrimony. One aspect of the Whistle which I had not clearly perceived before, was that most of the men were separated from their wives, and bitterly skilled in the fine shades of desertion while others were as yet unmarried. With Evelyn gone there was no feminine brake and maleness gathered speed. I think the number of customers rose and it was not all due to the weather; it was male liberty-hall at the Whistle. There should have been a shrine to Priapus above the board with the licensee's name.

One female, however, escaped the general wrath at this time. Mrs. Milligan, the landlady of The Three Humble Cheeses, an inn on the road to Pilney, took charge of the Whistle one night while Alf played away in a darts team. Mrs. Milligan was big and rosy and wore tight silk dresses. She could be more dirty-minded than the men; was kind-hearted and an authority on what horses to bet, so she was quite a favourite. She was especially severe on Evelyn.

"Any woman," said Mrs. Milligan inflamed and indignant, "who would leave her two young kids for a thing like Norman Povis must be soft in the head or a bloody villain. I wouldn't want him in my bed. Would you?" She addressed me sharply.

"Lord no. Alf's quite attractive in a James Mason way," said I.

"She's a bloody villain," said Mrs. Milligan, "or she's soft in the head."

One Saturday afternoon when Frank was not free and I was to start work at six, I called at my parents' house. They had gone out for the day to one of the neighbouring large towns to pay some bills, shop and perhaps see a film, but Jessie was at home using the washing-machine in the kitchen. I sat on a chair chatting as she wrung the clothes through the wringer. The house was quiet about us, the birds' songs drifting m In a long mirror propped slant-wise inside the window above the row of groups, one had a view of the garden and any goat that might dare to sneak in for a mouthful of blossom. Jessie had explained that my mother had rigged up the mirror device and was pleased with her idea. It also enabled her to keep track of any human trespassers too. Jessie spoke mainly of local people and the small news of the district, all of which was very much on the periphery of my interest at present, but there is a pleasure for members of a family in summoning again old names and present fortunes, and Jessie's happy nature delighting in her friends' marriages and babies seemed to take the gloom out of the universe. There was a quality of innocence about her that I re-saw and appreciated each time I saw her.

She had dried her hands and suggested I go into the garden with her and take some of the fruit as there was such a glut this year. I was following her when I noticed the ring. It was lying on the draining-board, the same that I had once seen on her hand during Sunday

44

dinner. "Your ring, Why!" I said, admiring, "these look like real sapphires. What a beauty it is."

"Harry gave it to me," she said. "Yes, they are real sapphires, John." There was a wistfulness in her voice, if wistfulness is the right word, for it was not only the tone of her voice but the look in her eyes and the very way that she breathed just then that communicated sadness to me. Yet the sadness was on my part, not hers. Harry was her employer, a handsome out-of-doors type of man in his early forties. From the way my sister had spoken I knew now that she loved him. I could not have been mistaken: I too was a victim. But at least Frank and I had reached our triumphant conclusion. I knew it was not so with my sister. So many young men had admired her but she had had eyes for none of them. It was a really bitter jest of fate that she should fall in love with Harry Devereaux. Not that the gap in age mattered much: there were few men so honourable or intelligent, and he had wealth and looks. But he was married. He had been separated from his wife for some years.

I wondered how much my mother knew. It seemed that she would see neither of her children married, for Harry's wife received such a liberal allowance from him and was too sworn against divorce ever to give or pursue grounds for one. I foresaw that my sister would waste the sweetest part of her life, and nothing seemed—or seems—a more wretched life to me than a life without fulfilled love.

It was with a sense of doom approaching for my family that, laden with fruit, I left for work. I could bear that the world would be merciless in its scorn of me for I knew the way God had knitted and twisted me in the beginning and I could be no other, but I could not bear that Jessie should have to suffer the cruelty of tongues or practise on herself the blasphemy and self-murder of stifling love which is the inward sun of human life.

CHAPTER EIGHT

It was the end of Summer. The glorious days, with Frank constantly present and supporting me with his strength and joyfulness, had lulled me. Even if our relationship had to be kept secret, I had never been so happy. For a while I forgot the possibility of unhappiness. In what I must call my single days, I had taken a pleasure in the splendid decay of Autumn, when Hawkward Wood was afire with falling beech-leaves and the sun set on the moors in a solemn glow like the end of the world itself. But now I was out of patience with the wilfulness of the seasons; a continuing summer would have accorded more with my inner disposition.

Evelyn had not returned to her children or husband at the Whistle, though she had 'phoned twice from a 'phone-box in the manufacturing city, to ask how the kids were. The Whistle thus continued in its forlorn state with Alf glooming and the volunteer helps being inexperienced. It was rumoured that Alf might pack in his licence before Christmas and take a job as a foundry-man in another district. The pub was rather empty too at this back-end of the year, when bad weather had not yet driven young men in and many in the building trade were working on jobs which took them out of the immediate district.

Late one afternoon not long after I had just risen for breakfast, for I had worked the previous night and was due to start again at seven, there was a playing of fingers on the door of the flat and I admitted Frank. He had a duplicate key which I had given him but this he had left in his best suit. He was wearing ragged jeans and was unshaven. As he was usually very careful about his appearance I would have assumed that he was working, except that when he was in work he was cheerful. There was a gloom and unease about him that

46

told me he was between jobs. He sat in broody silence. I put a piece of music on, the volume turned low, so that any words of ours might be under cover from the attentive ears of Miss Bee. This was a now reflex action with me, as if I were living under the Gestapo, but as in my lonely days I had heard Miss Bee cough in her apartment it was just possible that some of my conversation was likewise blown down ventilation shafts and old chimney-passages to my vigilant neighbour.

"I met the old girl near the stairs," said Frank. "I told her I'd come to see about the chairs."

"The chairs?" I was nonplussed. "She knows I have all these new cane chairs."

"You could be selling them, couldn't you?" he said crossly.

"Yes, but if I remember rightly you said you were looking after the boiler the last time."

"Oh what the hell has it got to do with her, anyway? The old trout should feed her canary and not go nosing. Can you lend me some money?"

Now I had exactly ten shillings.

"My mother's raising the hell and says I can get out if I don't give her something," he went on. I knew that Mrs. Jeffers believed in keeping her son up to scratch in the matter of his responsibilities. "And I've got to pay that fine for the bike, and I'm not due for the dole because I walked out when that sod...."

"What fine?" I demanded. "What bike?"

"It'll be in this week's 'Advertiser'. I didn't tell you because you're like my mam. The pair of you carry on so. It was Jimmy Dawson's bike. Anyway it's only five pounds. But that can wait. It's a pair of trousers I want. I can't get a job in these."

"Frank," I said. "I've only got ten shillings. Why in heaven's name do you have to go borrowing bikes, if it was a borrow?"

"Listen here, mush," said Frank angrily. "It wasn't borrowed. Jimmy Dawson was on it with me. You can ask him."

"Honest, Frank, you're an idiot. You go getting yourself wrong with the police for such stupid petty things, and you pay in the long run, when I'm not with you..."

"Now just shut up. I've had enough from my mam."

"And you never told us. I suppose Hurley ran you in?"

"Yes, the sod. I offered to fight him but he wouldn't take his helmet off. He knows I can beat him."

I supposed the truth was even worse than he was telling me. "When do you have to pay the fine?"

"Nine tomorrow."

"Well, I can't help you now. But tomorrow..."

"I'm not worrying about the rozzers. My mother says she'll throw my shirts in the street. What's left of them."

"Left of them? You can stay here tonight. What difference does it make? I'll get some money tomorrow; you can pay her something on account and pay the fine off. As for trousers, you can wear mine.'"

"You've such a graceful little arse," he said with a grin, "they wouldn't go near me."

"Well, I've got to get washed and shaved."

While I was out of sight in the bathroom he plucked up courage. Slowly, ashamedly, jerkily, he told me of the unholy row that had taken place in the Jeffers household. The maternal curses (well deserved in my opinion after learning about the fire) I took as being Frank's translation into his robuster style. Mrs. Jeffers had thrown all his clothes into a suitcase and told him to leave the house at once. There was a pause outside the bathroom door.

"You do annoy her, Frank," I said as if to state a fair case for the opposition as I started on my chin.

"I was a bit wild," Frank began again. "So—well—like—I chucked the case on the fire."

I cut myself.

"And the whole damn thing went up in a blaze. If you tried to light a suitcase, it wouldn't," he said bitterly. "I meant it as, as a gesture, but my effing shirts and my best suit went up in a mushroom cloud."

I came out of the bathroom with bits of toilet paper stuck on my shaving wounds.

"And," said Frank solemnly, "the chimney came down—tons of soot. Mam screamed and rapped for those buggers next door; if they didn't play darts all night on the bedroom wall we'd have had a bit of sleep and none of this would have happened. So when you heard the sirens it was for our house."

"Honest to God!" I exclaimed, and saw the time. "Really, Frank!"

"I expected a bit of sympathy," he said sulkily. "I know I shouldn't have done it, but I did."

"You're a swine to your mother." I thought of the Swiss and Dutch ornaments covered in soot. "You're like a lunatic."

"Yes, I know," he agreed.

"And the key to the flat was in your best suit when it went on the fire?"

"Yes."

"Listen, Frank. I'll have to rush off. You stay here. There isn't much in to eat but I'll bring some chops back in the morning. There's enough for tonight. We can straighten things out tomorrow. There isn't a bus so I'll have to dash."

"No," he said obstinately. "I'll go in with you."

"Whatever for?" I argued, struggling into my coat. "You'll only make things worse if you go quarrelling with your mother. Stay here."

"No, I can't stay doing nothing."

"There's the gramophone."

"That old corn." He dismissed classical music, which I left undefended. We sped out together, unspeaking. As we covered the distance under the trees and then along the streets, the sense of urgency left me when I knew I would be in time for work, and I became more aware of him soundlessly at my side. He was wearing thick plimsolls and his feet made no sound. Seeing his soft burglar tread I had a sudden dread. I stopped and seized him by the collar. We were in the light of a shop window and people looked at us curiously.

"Frank," I urged, "please don't do anything silly."

"What do you mean?" he said roughly.

49

"You know what I mean. I can straighten things out tomorrow. It just isn't worth the time in prison for the money you get. And you've never been successful." I was keeping my voice low. "At least bank-robbers get thousands of pounds but all you can steal is a few pounds, and you're always caught too, and next time you may not get prison but be hung. It's bound to happen one day that someone will disturb you—you'll give him a blow, and then you'll be hung. Please go back to the flat, Frank."

"You're a proper little law-abiding rabbit," he sneered; "I'm not going to be hung."

"I bet that's what they all said." My worst fears were confirmed. I could see that my words about hanging had half-impressed him, but in the light of the shop window I could see that not only was he smiling—perhaps I did sound funny—but there was also a shining in his eyes. A sort of excitement. Here was the eager brightness of a schoolboy about to play truant and go for a day's swimming.

"Please don't come into the town," I begged again.

He laughed and shook my hand off, and I felt it was useless. I had to hurry. There was a mist coming up the streets, the houses seemed to be more decaying as the year died. At one of the corners he stopped. "I won't see you to the works. I'll drop in tomorrow. Be good, Johnny," and with a wave he was gone.

I did my work more from habit than anything else, the mechanical side of my brain carrying on, while all the time I kept on worrying and torturing myself. With only ten shillings he was not likely to get so drunk that he would sally forth to provoke P.C. Hurley. But it would be so easy for him to fall from a drainpipe or crash through a glass roof, or some innocent household might justifiably resent his presence. I imagined the court scene, the death cell. And serve him right, I told myself; he deserves to be hung.

Every time the policeman on his nightly beat passed the yards at Barraclough's I found myself waiting and listening, as if the entire police force would break into a run and chase at news of Frank's burglary.

50

Gradually I argued myself into believing that I had imagined the expression in Frank's eyes. He would be tired of my nagging him, and a laugh would be his natural reaction if he had not been meaning mischief. He had not been engaged in any thieving activity while I had known him. Surely he would not be stupid enough to risk his freedom for the sake of a few doubtful pounds.

Just after eleven the telephone rang and guiltily I recognised Henry Robinson's voice. I was supposed to have rung him earlier about some haulage contracting, but I had completely forgotten. He sounded full of excitement. "Sorry you couldn't get us earlier, old man, but we've been having a lively time here; the police asked the Exchange not to put calls through. We didn't want the burglar to be disturbed." He paused triumphantly.

"Burglar?" I said faintly.

"Better make sure you have some good alarms at your place," Henry chatted on. "I never knew there were so many criminals in Hawkward, before tonight. You should have seen this fellow—a real tough. I was passing the offices when I thought I heard a noise. I crept up to the keyhole and as luck happened the light of a passing car showed him up. I got the police on the downstairs line. They were really wonderful, caught him redhanded. He was after the safe, of course, but there was nothing in it. It's not been used for years. Milly kept her jam and a bit of food there, out of the way of the flies."

I was absolutely convinced now that the burglar was Frank.

"I suppose I'm lucky to be alive," said Henry complacently. "If I'd gone in... Such a brute. The police said he'd been a boxer, with a record as long as your arm. It took them long enough to overpower him. Bold as brass too. He said he'd just dropped in for a pee. With a screwdriver in his pocket." Henry laughed.

"Where is he now?"

"Getting wopped at the cop-shop, I expect. And I don't blame them from the way he spoke to them. It opens one's eyes, that sort of thing."

"I suppose he'll get bail?"

"I don't know. A fellow like that—they'll surely hold him to see what else he's been doing. The sergeant said that these lone wolves are always the worst....And I'll have to appear as a witness," purred Henry.

I sat glum and crushed, angry and helpless. Who would go bail for Frank—but was it Frank? If I acted as surety, it would look suspicious, or would it? I felt ill with confusion. But there was Robinson to be got rid of, I could hear him bleating in the telephone. I picked up the list of deliveries for our firm.

"I'm sorry, Henry," I said. "Have you any spare wagons for tomorrow? Good..."

I was confused and anxious all though the night. In my clearer moments I told myself that I was being stupid, for after all Frank might not have broken into Robinson's at all and I would see him the same as usual in the evening. But in the morning I wandered near the police station in the hope that I might see someone who knew whether Frank was implicated or not. The outside of the police station gave me no information. I did not know whether he was inside or not.

At seven o'clock that morning I had received a 'sub' from the cashier and so I stopped at the butcher's, who opened early for the morning workers and I bought two steaks. In the new day it seemed that I had let my imagination run away with me. Frank was probably waiting for me in or near the flat, for he was experienced enough to get in even without a key, and he would be starving. I chose the very best steaks.

My heart rose in jubilance as I approached the flat; I was more and more convinced that he would be there. I hurried up the stairs. The flat was sleeping. I crossed to the bedroom and looked at the bed, but there was only the emptiness and silence of the rooms. Like a blow, disappointment hit me. I lay on the bed wishing I could be unborn and finally in sheer hopelessness fell asleep.

I could not be certain and I wanted some news of what had happened. On the way to work that night I set out early and went along the street where Frank's mother lived. There were streaks of soot on the pavement but no sign of Mrs. Jeffers. I didn't like to knock at the door. It was then I turned my steps to the Whistle. They would know there, as they knew everything, or Frank himself might be there.

Some lorry-drivers were playing in the games-room, but at the bar there was only Alf. I invited him to have a drink and we spoke about the weather and the drawing-in of the nights. It was only at the second drink that he spoke suddenly: "I suppose you've heard about Frank Jeffers?"

I shook my head.

"He broke into Robinson's, the haulage firm. He'll get it in the neck this time, being caught red-handed. His mother was in here that night looking for him."

And now I was in here looking for him.

"I feel sorry for his mother," Alf went on. "Have you ever seen her—a little old girl, works like a trooper? But she's spoilt him. Not that he's bad. He just goes daft, like that time he went off with the steam-roller."

"He was drunk then," I put in.

"But he was planning to sell it for scrap. You hear a lot in here, but of course, you have to be just ears and make out you've heard nothing. He'd been upset then, though. It's as if that triggered him into doing a job."

"Where is he now?"

"Hugeley."

"Hugeley? I thought Pilney was the main police headquarters."

"Yes, but Robinson's is just over the border in Hugeley Town. There's a strip of Hugeley Town which runs right up to Hawkward. It makes things complicated. He'll be tried at Hugeley and go to Harmsworth Gaol. I reckon he'll be lucky to get three years this time."

"Don't you think he might get off?"

Alf showed a bit of gold tooth. He gazed at me for a while.

"Between you and me," said Alf, confidentially, "you'll be better off without him. He's a bent penny, that lad."

It was true, but unconsoling, as if I had told Alf in turn that he was better off without Evelyn. What is evident to reason so often has no conviction for the heart. The prospect of three years friendless without Frank turned me to nothing.

CHAPTER NINE

"Well, for God's sake say something."

I had not spoken a word to him since Frank had suddenly appeared from the doorway of the closed dry cleaners' next to the fish and chip shop, opposite the hatchery. After so many days of not seeing him or touching him, I had in fact felt excitement and a molten tenderness at his unexpected presence, but I did not want my first words to be those of affection any more than I wanted them to be a whine at his conduct.

"If you're going to take it like this then I'd better scarper," he growled, but still kept at my side. For all his fierceness I could sense that he was ashamed and in a way frightened. "It was only a bit of..."

"I don't know what you expect me to say," I cut in, "but I hope your mother has said it. Breaking into Robinson's wasn't a bit, it was a good sized piece of dirty work. And it was so pointless when I could have got the money for you the next day. I only hope you see a psychiatrist this time in prison."

"Me a mental case?" he said indignantly. "I don't wear ear-rings."

"Your ears are too hairy," I said. "Anyway, I've never stolen."

"They haven't proved I have—yet," he declared virtuously.

"But they will. You haven't a leg to stand on."

"You're a fat lot of comfort, and I don't think." His face was set and moody.

"It's going to rain," I said miserably.

"Have you any money?"

"I've heard that one before." I intended to make the remark lightly, but it got Frank on the raw.

"You're a sarky, snotty bugger, and I feel like punching you through that window. I asked because I've just enough for a half-pint each, and that money you hear rattling isn't mine, it's for two fish my mam sent me out to buy, only I thought I'd like to see you, you sarky sod."

"Wouldn't you like to come to the flat?"

"Yes, but I can't. My mother won't let me out of her sight. I'm on bail and it's hell. I'll be glad to be in the nick after this. We'll have one drink and then I'll have to whip back with a couple of fish."

Amicably we went to take shelter in the Whistle.

The noise of the juke-box shielded us from eavesdroppers as we sat in the singing-room.

"He's a bit of a drip, my solicitor," Frank said. "He's young and doesn't know much. He thought at first I should plead guilty."

"Well, so you are," said I.

"What?" Frank was surprised. "Now don't be ignorant. I wasn't at the safe, Johnny. They may be able to prove breaking-in. I may have been on premises with unlawful intent, but that's what those pasty-faced pot-bellied lot have to prove. And what's the evidence? One screwdriver. Can't a fellow carry a screwdriver in his pocket?"

My silence was sceptical, but Frank was too rapt to notice.

"That yard wasn't private. There was no notice to say so. There could have been plenty of reasons for me to go in. Say, I thought a cat was trapped in there. Would they have liked the cat to die—dying slowly?"

"And I suppose you were going to pee in the safe?"

"Whose side are you on, mine or the police?" asked Frank, exasperated.

"I think you've had it, Frank. Nobody is going to believe that there was a cat, or if there were, that you would have cared a brass button."

"I rescued a boy from the canal once," he said defensively, and became pensive. I ordered two more pints.

"Did you get a medal?"

"No. But it was in the papers."

After a pause, not to see him looking so downhearted, I said, "That could be mentioned in your favour."

"It's about the only bloody thing," he said ruefully. He had become deeply dejected. "How long do you think I'll get, Johnny?"

"The maximum."

He fired up at this as if I had given a deadly insult. "It's a wonder you have your face." I could see him thinking. "I did save that kid from drowning. I could do with a few blokes speaking in my favour. I must have some good points. You think I have some good points, don't you, Johnny? Couldn't you come and speak in my favour?"

"If I spoke about the good points I like you for," I said in alarm, "I'd be arrested myself. What difference would it make to you breaking into Robinson's if I told the judge I loved your big white teeth and your hair. It wouldn't do you any good at all."

"All you have to do," said Frank, "is say you've known me for ages and I've been of good character."

"Well, Frank."

"What do you mean, 'Well, Frank.' What's wrong with my character?"

I was at a loss how to put it delicately.

"What's wrong with my mucking character?" demanded Frank fiercely. "I thought you loved me."

"Keep your hair on, I do. I didn't mean there was anything wrong with your character. It's just that you're Unbalanced."

"Oh," said Frank, mollified.

"It's a waste of time sending you to prison."

"It is that," said Frank feelingly and with interest.

"Because you thieve again when you're out. And your robberies are plain daft. Taking that steam-roller, for instance. Even this last business. I think the motive was more for excitement and relief of tension than straightforward robbery. It's a waste of money sending you to prison. You should be in the hands of a psychiatrist. You would be in Sweden."

"I'm a bit of a nut-case, then?" Frank enquired with humble interest. He looked pleased.

"Yes, I think so."

"I must say you've the gift of the gab, Johnny. You and the vicar will strengthen my case."

"What's the vicar got to do with it?"

"The vicar? I'm one of his parishioners, aren't I?"

"But you've never been to church in your life!"

"I went last Sunday, and I used to go to Sunday-school—least, I was supposed to. Anyway, I had a talk with the old boy afterwards. He gave me a glass of port," said Frank with relish. "That was at the vicarage. He's coming along to testify. He says it was the strain of my health that got me into temptation."

"Your health? You? Why, you're like a bull elephant."

"Don't be such a cluck, Johnny. What's the point of having a trial if I make no defence? And I dug those graves for them cheap—anyone else would have wanted more than a quid. When you do a good turn," said Frank virtuously, "you get your reward in the long run, I think he'll go down well with the magistrate, white hair and very lah-de-dah, you know. Mind you, I'm supposed to have turned over a new leaf so I don't want to be seen in here with you."

"Thanks," I said.

"Not that the old boy's likely to come in here. He's got all the booze he wants in his own house."

"I don't like your just making use of him," I said, rather awkwardly, for I felt ashamed as if Frank were cowardly. "You don't sound as if you respect him."

Frank was silent for a while, then he lit a cigarette. "I do respect him. You're wrong there. It's only the way I talk. It's like this, Johnny. I haven't any time for church and that crap. I'm just an ordinary fellow. But this old boy's genuine and kind, he wants to help and I need help. There's only him and you, and my mam, but she'll be no use in court. Won't you help me, Johnny?"

I was full of misgivings. But Frank gazed at me with his clear strong eyes; he was in deadly earnest. He was appealing to me and relying on me. It seemed to me that should I appear in court the nature of our relationship would be plain to all in the court-room.

But at the worst, this would merely mean that I would follow him to prison. It was a small price to pay for the fulfilment he had brought me. I was prepared to die for him, so that a loss of reputation would be a minor sacrifice.

"Yes; I'll help you," I said.

"Would you have a talk with the old boy? He kept asking if I had any honest friends. I could only think of Len Shaw and he's a proper bloody crook. Could you come to my mam's before one on Saturday and we could go up to the vicarage together. Will you, Johnny? You use the sort of words he does."

Well, I would have preferred going to the vicarage with him for the banns to be put up, but I could, if Frank had been whitewashing himself too much, at least save the vicar from being imposed on. I had the feeling too, that a priest might be well-read enough in human nature to be of true assistance to Frank. No doubt I obscurely hoped that perhaps he might be of assistance to me also. If I were to encounter the full force of society's contempt and persecution I would need an uncommon spiritual stoicism and an unshaken faith that our love was worth the world.

CHAPTER TEN

As it happened, I never did go to the vicarage. On the Saturday, Milton asked several of us to stay back so that important orders for Italy could be cleared. "Phone and put it off," was all he said gruffly when I brought up my having an engagement. After that there was nothing I could do; it had taken some resolution to mention at all that I was disinclined to work over.

If I did not turn up, Frank would interpret it as desertion on my part. There was no way to get in touch with him directly. At eleven I rang the Whistle on the off-chance that he might be there. Alf answered. No, Frank Jeffers was not at the bar. Did I know that his case was coming up on Monday?

I hadn't known that the trial was to be so soon and this made me all the more anxious to avoid letting Frank feel that I had abandoned him. I asked Alf if he could take a message for me to Frank's house. But there was only himself in the bar, Alf told me, and Peggotty. I had not thought that the state of Peggotty's mentality would ever be of importance in my life. He was a half-imbecile youth (actually he was thirty but he looked sixteen) whose suggestibility was such that once, on being told to go and smash the bank's windows, he had done so. He had been given six months in prison for that, and he had teetered on the edge of crime ever since.

"I'd leave the bar and go for you if it was anyone else but him," said Alf, "but I can't trust him alone in here. He takes a swig out of all the liquors."

I did not relish trusting Peggotty with a message, but I knew he must have some memory, as he collected his dole with no forgetfulness every week.

"Well, he likes to help," said Alf, "and I'd write the message down for him to give it. I can watch from the door to make sure he goes in the right direction."

I dictated a message which was written down and given to Peggotty. But with such a weak-winged messenger I afterwards remained in doubt as to whether it had arrived at the Jeffers' house.

Monday came. I had worked through the night and on returning to the flat I set the alarm clock to wake me in four hours. Frank's case was to be heard in the afternoon, but I was not certain of the time and still did not know if he had received my message.

I woke at half-past one and washed, shaved and dressed in a hurry. It was a good hour's bus ride to Hugeley. Trust Frank to break into a building that came under the jurisdiction of the Hugeley police. Crimes in Hawkward proper were tried at Pilney, a shorter ride away. By bad luck the bus I got on was of the single-decker, infinitely-stopping variety—we had two companies running services to Hugeley and the ride took over an hour. Four o'clock found me wandering in the sooty centre of Hugeley. There was a town-hall, a depressing looking museum and municipal offices flanked by stone mermen, bearded, but otherwise sexless, who carried globe-like gas lamps in their hands. I realised I had riot the faintest idea where the courts of law were, or even what they were called—assizes or petty sessions. Such legal expertise had not been required of me till Frank loomed into my life. After wandering on aimlessly, with the winter dusk coming and a few stars piercing the pale end of day, I plucked up courage and asked a policeman. He was a big, beautiful-skinned, depraved looking specimen of a man and he surveyed me with a broad understanding grin. This increased my embarrassment, particularly as he seemed reluctant to let me go, as if he wanted me to keep on chatting with him. But thanks to his expansiveness I learnt that most of the cases for the day had already been tried, and the court-house was half-an-hour away at the other side of the town. I did not feel up to entertaining the police and was becoming more tense as the policeman became more affable. I had the impression he had been a sergeant in the army. With someone else coming to ask for directions I was able to get away, but not before the policeman had told me that the early cases would be reported in that evening's local newspaper.

I wished I had brought an overcoat; it was becoming cold. The evening dailies were not on sale yet and I wandered about, looking in jewellers' windows. The streets began filling up with people hurrying home from work. Soon the pubs would be open and the evening editions on sale. I went into a herbalist's shop and had a lingering drink of hot peppermint for fourpence. When I came out it was almost five. I joined the surging crowds making to the buses in a side street. At the corner an old fellow in a tattered raincoat was selling papers. I bought the local evening paper and glanced rapidly at the front page, but there wasn't a word about Frank. An Irish labourer who had knocked down a policeman in a terrific family row shared the limelight with tension over Berlin. I could not examine the inside of the paper on such a crowded corner. I drifted along in search of a pub, a quiet one. Most of them looked already packed, with moving shadows seen through the frosted glass and more hot-faced stained men pushing inside.

I came again among the municipal buildings now ebbing of life. At the corner there was a dignified high-class place with an awning over the pavement. With my paper I went inside. The roof was all of stained glass. The lights were low and the chairs were of leather with Gothic-looking arms and backs. I wondered faintly why a pub should be given a Pugin flavour. I was the only customer and sat with my mediaeval-looking tankard and read the paper in the dim light while the crow-faced barmaid coloured her nails. There were dozens of cases; the courts must have had a busy day. I skimmed the opening phrases "Patrick ...twenty-three years...of no fixed abode, labourer... grievous bodily harm. P.C. Derman..." They were all quite young, nearly all labourers. The sentences ranged from six months to three years. It felt even more depressing in the murky light. I came on Frank on the fourth page and nearly missed him in the unfamiliar aspect of 'Francis William Jeffers...labourer.' I had not known he had a middle name. There followed an accurate description of the accused having been found with a screwdriver in his pocket before the office safe on the premises of Messrs. Robinson. My eyes rushed to the lower paragraphs. The magistrates in imposing an eighteen months' sentence stated that but for the plea made on the accused's behalf by the Reverend Edgar Lumley they would have imposed a severer penalty. My eyes went to the middle paragraphs where the Reverend Edgar Lumley stated that the accused, whom he had always known to be a good worker, had recently got into financial difficulties through poor health. He felt that the accused had been led into error by frequenting public houses.

I sat numb, working out how old Frank would be when he came out, how old I would be....I felt relief that it was not three years, but more, I felt exasperation that he should have committed such a stupid little crime. I expected that with his usual cheerfulness he was probably enjoying himself wherever he was; more than I was alone in this mediaeval museum. At least there would be three in the cell. Then I remembered how he had half-boasted, half-cried, that no prison would hold him if there was a next time. But he had been free then; big talk was easy. Faced with the reality of state authority he would knuckle under and become the tamest of trusties.

I felt utterly empty. I had no aim or hope in life except him, and now the wall of Warmley Prison stood blocking my life.

I left the Pugin-like pub and walked around the cold brilliantly lit streets in a dreary daze before I caught a bus back to Hawkward.

I was glad I had not seen him sentenced.

CHAPTER ELEVEN

For some weeks I did not go near the Whistle. At work we were busy preparing a big advertisement campaign for next Easter. I kept on working the irregular system of nights, afternoons and days. With the night working, my eyes were too tired to read once I reached home; my only relaxations were sleep and music. But every sort of music was too sad and only sent me into a passive despair; even the cheerful hit-tunes which I bought to bring some brightness seemed to become pathetic in their stridency when listened to in solitude. Outside was the dirt and darkness of early winter, only working occasionally at night in the office, I would see the moon in a bare sky over Hawkward—the one beautiful thing it seemed in the universe.

I knew I was neglecting my parents, but I felt too depressed to encounter them very often. On the telephone I forced myself to cheerfulness. My mother perpetually urged me to keep myself warm and avoid draughts at the office at night. Desperately I would hunt for topics to talk about so that her anxiousness for my winter comfort would not take up such a disproportionate part of our conversation. I was always conscious of a large vacuum in our communication —that part where my affections lay and where other sons would speak to their mothers about wives and children.

With my days in this condition of dull undrinking despair, I was astonished one morning of sharp blueness and rare feeble sunshine, to run into Alf Barnes, Evelyn and the two girls. The last I had heard of Evelyn was her deserting her husband for Norman Povis; now she must, I guessed, have deserted Norman Povis in his turn. The little girls were in smart new winter coats. Evelyn wore a grave, settled, matronly expression and was a bit subdued in manner. Alf looked dominant, confident and beaming, as if he had won all his bets. He wore a crisply ironed shirt which looked strange on him after his months of rumpled tie-lessness.

"It's good to see you, Johnny," was all that Evelyn said, in a sad low voice and with a nervous smile. She stood looking downcast, a little apart with the girls pulling at her coat and being reprimanded, while Alf very obviously explaining her reappearance drew me to the centre of the pavement.

"She came back for her clothes," said Alf pithily, "or that's the tale. That bugger had had enough of her—it's a different tale when you have to pay for her brandies. I was thinking of the kids, and who misses a slice from the loaf? That's what I told myself. Mind you, I didn't say yes straight away. I kept her on tenterhooks a bit—we stayed up till six talking, but she could see I wouldn't say no. The only thing is," said Alf looking fiercely around the street, "is that that bugger is back here in Hawkward, and shooting his mouth off about the time he had with her. There's only him and me knows about them things with her and they're bloody lies most of them. Well, I can't put up with that, Johnny, and I'll have to have it out with him—man to man. He's all lard and I reckon I've a powerful weight behind my fist. But he's lying low, the rat. I've never clapped eyes on him once, though every morning it's dry we come out for a stroll. I'm bound to meet him in the end. Our tracks," said Alf with solemn menace, "are bound to cross, and then by God help him!"

After a suitable pause he turned to me. "You've not been coming in. Frank?"

I nodded.

"The lads have been missing you." He mentioned names. I was surprised and a little flattered that the weekday blue jeans (with best suits on Saturdays) had noticed my absence or even my presence. "They were saying the other night that you'd be a bit on the lonely side now, and none of them had seen you. They reckon you've had a bad penny in Frank Jeffers—not that any of them are angels, come to that, but Frank's a bit of a screwball. They were only saying they were surprised a good-looking young fellow like you went with him when you could have had a better time with, well, a more dependable bloke. They liked the way you stuck to him, though. Many of them would have been only too glad, but Jeffers would have knocked their teeth in, and you never gave no encouragement. No, they respect that in a man," he noticed Evelyn and became grim, "or a woman. It's unusual. Mind you, I've the kids to put first. It's no use getting excited. But I'll flatten that bastard's nose yet."

This meeting, and either the rare sunshine or the sight of Alf's cheerfulness after his months of solitary gloom, rather brightened me. As he went on with his family he pressed me to drop in at the Whistle soon, and I promised that I would. But perhaps what raised my spirits was more Alf's suggestion that the young men had been noticing and studying me at the Whistle all the time I had been there with Frank. I had not suspected it, and of course, I was flattered. It was a revelation to me that among the young male population of the pub others could feel for another man the way that Frank and I did. They were attractive, strong and handsome. Not that I wanted another lover, for I wished only to wait till Frank returned, but I did feel in need of friends. In that morning conversation Alf had sown the seed of the idea that I had, or might have, friends at the old Pole and Whistle.

Even so, it was some weeks before I finally ventured into the Whistle alone, and I would probably not have gone then but for its being a Friday night. I had the evening free; it was crisp and cold with a feeling that snow might come before morning; I felt restless and tired of my own company and the records in the flat.

The records on the juke-box had been changed since my last visit; now 'Cupid, Draw Your Bow' was hammering its decibels in the ears of the crowded pub. I was warmly greeted, and also had pints bought for me by the old inner aristocracy (or inmates) of the place, such as Les Barron, Neil Crossley and Tommy Dunkin. I was not too pleased at being accosted in such a friendly way by Les Barron, for I thought he had been a wrong influence upon Frank. But he was very charming, and handsome too in a South American way. He always had a great deal of money, more than he could earn as an electrician, I suspected, and was surrounded by friends. I would not have chosen to be drawn into his orbit, but after refusing several invitations to his table, the nearest to the fire, I gave way and moved to a seat beside him. It was embarrassing sitting alone, and if I had refused once more I felt he would take it as an insult. Drinks disappeared quickly at this table. Barron dropped a hand negligently on my leg. In next to no time the drink had made me cosy and happy. I heard myself talking merrily, and casually I got rid of the hand, but it returned—with more strength. I pretended not to notice; after all, I thought, one of us would have to leave for the toilet sooner or later. After waiting I was forced to go first, but there was no escape as Barron simply followed me. As the door of the gents swung back he kissed me, drawing me close. There were young men standing at the stalls, watching us with a sort of dull curiosity. Perhaps they were used to such scenes.

"I'll give you a good time," Barron said. "Better than Frank could. Oh, he's a nice lad but he's never been with a woman. You'll know yourself after you've been with me."

I didn't want to commit myself, but I didn't want to offend him. He was a strong and rather brutal man. Though Frank, who was stronger, had sometimes spoken of hitting me, he had never done so, even at his most angry, but I had no doubt that Barron would hit me if I enraged him. I came back with him, feeling like a prisoner. Probably seeing me look tense and sullen, Les changed his tactics—anyway he seemed to become pleasanter. I forgot that others were looking at us. Fresh drinks kept coming all the time, brought mostly by Alf. Evelyn sat down and had a drink with us at one time. I think she was very fond of Les herself, but knew that after her recent escapade she must watch her behaviour. He noticed that I was looking at him and smiled at me, sure of himself and me. The thought of Frank still kept me detached.

Closing time came but this merely meant that the curtains were drawn more closely and the front door closed. It had been ascertained that the local police force was busy with parking and admission at a political dinner and was not fussing about the pubs tonight. There was a flurry and scurry as the more early-rising or law-abiding wished to be let out, the parties leaving by a side door in the residential part of the pub. Barron's attention wandered from me for a moment and I decided to step out unobtrusively with one of the departing groups who passed our table at that moment. The manoeuvre was successful. I found myself in the cold air, my head clearing, and began walking to the flat. Whereas I loved Frank, with all his defects, Barron's attraction for me was purely sensual. I was glad to have escaped the temptation even if only by flight. I told myself I must not go to the Whistle again.

There was a queue at the chip-shop. I left the lights of the centre behind me, the houses where people were going to bed, and passed into the silent road with the bare trees. A lonely dog slunk into the darkness.

The headlights of a car lit up the road in front of me. I heard men's voices shouting. I turned as a long grey car drew alongside. Barron was out, holding me by the hands.

"That wasn't very nice, Johnny."

Harry, in blue jeans and a sweater, was driving the car. He had been at our table at the Whistle.

"I wanted you to have supper. There's no need to be shy."

"Frank," I began.

"He'd rather you had a friend. Come on, Johnny. You're a bit sweet on me, aren't you now? Aren't you?" And it was true. He was a different type physically from Frank but as I saw him in the beam from the car—his shining black hair, olive-brown skin and brutal good looks and felt the compact warmth and taut thrust of his body, I let him lead me willingly, wanting to be wanted, to the back seat of the car. Harry said nothing during the drive to Les' house but gave me a wink as we got out. Apparently he was going to use the car, which was Les', to take a girl out and park it later in the yard opposite.

We heard him do so, the lights sweeping across the bedroom ceiling, and the keys rattle through the letter-box. Barron was spirited and overpowering. We did not rise till after one o'clock on the

Sunday. He made me breakfast and I went straight to work from his house.

One night not long after this, as I was returning from work, I met Mrs. Jeffers in the street and carried her basket some way for her. She had been shopping at the Co-op after a day's work. She looked tired, old and unwell to me.

"It's a shame you have to work," I said clumsily. She was such a frail little woman to do a long day's work at her age. I thought she might be having money troubles and if I had known how to set about it tactfully would have offered help.

"It's the best thing. I couldn't stay all day in the house," she replied in a sad voice. "The job takes my mind off things."

"Have you been to see Frank?"

"He wouldn't like it." After a pause she said bitterly, "He hasn't been so good to me, Johnny? He's been a bad son. It could have been so different. We were none of us wild. I don't know what will happen to him when I'm gone."

We walked on. Her face was drawn, in the light from the street lamp she looked ghastly.

"You want to look after yourself," I said cheerfully.

"I'm going to bed straight after a cup of tea. I don't feel like T.V. tonight."

At the corner of the street she took the basket. "He loves you," she said in a low voice. "He pays attention to what you say. I only wish you could put up with him. He'll never change. No," said Mrs. Jeffers, "he'll never change for me. But he just might for you."

I was astonished and impressed. I didn't know what to say and then she was gone. It was as if she had entrusted her son to me, and I had already broken faith. I vowed I would see no more of Les Barron, if I could.

CHAPTER TWELVE

It was at the Whistle some weeks later (during one of my relapses) that I learnt Frank had been in Hawkward—or rather, to the neighbouring hilltop. Mrs. Jeffers had died and he had been given permission to attend her funeral. Everyone at the Whistle seemed to know about it, but to me, who had not been near the pub for a couple of weeks, the news was unexpected and shocking. I asked who was looking after the Jeffers' house now and was told that a female relation had come there and was making arrangements about the property. The tenancy was to be given up as soon as everything was settled. I presumed that he had sanctioned this disposal of the tenancy and his mother's belongings. I cursed again his inability to write; at least with a letter I would know how he felt. I might, too, have had a chance to see him on his escorted visit to the churchyard.

If he had known how to write, it might have given an outlet to his own feelings too. I was sure that now he would be brooding bitterly, the prison grown real to him at last.

The news and the realisation of what his mother's death would mean to him so disturbed me that I did not stay long at the Whistle. I lay in darkness at the flat. When at half-past eleven the buzzer of the new bell sounded time and time again, I did not get up to answer it. I had no time just then for Les Barron, for I guessed who it was. He would have heard about my going to the Whistle earlier that evening. The buzzer sounded imperiously again and again. I heard Miss Bee stirring, and then voices on the stairs. Then I heard his steps as he went away, and distantly a car door slammed.

I visited Mrs. Jeffers' grave on the Saturday. There was no stone but it was the newest grave there and on one of the already withered wreaths her name was written. The muddy earth had sunk in and there was a pool of water. I wished that I might never be interred but would die in a land where cremation was normal. The sky was sodden with yet more approaching rain. In that desolate place I felt extinct. I was haunted by that weary face in the lamp-lit winter street. I set down my own wreath, one of holly and quickly left the graveyard. I had half-intended to go to my parents', but the sight of the mud, the hollowed earth and rain-battered wreaths had depressed and chilled me too much for me to acquire a sudden cheerfulness before my parents. It was going to rain again soon. I took a bus down to Hawkward and the night closed in. Would the winter never end?

In my sleep I heard the knock. It must have been Miss Bee bumping a piece of furniture, I thought after a while. Later, the buzzer sounded, just once, mysteriously. I could not have been mistaken this time.

In slow motion I felt for the clock. It was four o'clock in the morning. Really, I thought, Les is going it a bit much. I hadn't heard him go away, yet the buzzer did not sound again. I was sure someone was there and lay waiting for a fresh sound. I heard nothing and the cheated expectancy brought me wide awake. I put the bedroom light on and went to the front door.

Instead of Barron, Frank stood there. He slipped inside at once and shot the bolt.

"Ssh!" he whispered, drawing me towards the lighted doorway. "Are you alone?"

"Yes."

"Draw the curtains in there."

"They're drawn."

"God! I'm cold."

He was in a big dirty mackintosh. His eyes were raw with lack of sleep, his skin white with exhaustion. His chin was bristly. I plugged the fires in as he lay back in an armchair.

"What's happened, Frank?"

"I've broken out, brother."

"Oh!" was all I could say.

71

He drew me to him, his hands icy. "Make me some grub in a bit." He ruffled my hair absent-mindedly.

"You look ghastly," I told him.

"You don't look so hot yourself—fix us up a bit of grub, Johnny. I can't wait."

I made him an instant soup which he wolfed with lots of bread, then I fried some bacon and black puddings. The red came into his cheeks, he became more animated and relaxed, drawing on a butt. There was only one cigarette in the flat (and that had belonged to Les Barron: he would smoke a bit then stub the cigarette out to linger out the enjoyment).

"Isn't there a machine nearby?" Frank asked irritably.

"Not for miles."

"I should have smashed one," he reproached himself.

"I'll go out as soon as the shops open," I promised.

"When do you begin work?"

"Noon."

"We might as well have a bit of kip then. Are you sure no one can get in?"

I reassured him, but he still worried.

"I hope the old girl doesn't hear us."

"She won't know who you are, but she can't hear in any case."

He stripped and rolled into bed beside me. He fell asleep almost at once but it was a little while before I dozed. I woke once to find him like a big cuddly bear about me and contentedly I slipped asleep again. Any worrying implications about his presence had as yet not appeared in my thoughts, but it occurred to me that I would have to tell him about Les Barron.

"That gipsy!" was all Frank said scornfully, when after a roundabout approach I confessed I had been seeing Barron. "I don't think much of your taste."

"He's quite handsome."

"He only wants you because he couldn't get that Wilcox girl." This was the most of his condemnation—to my considerable relief, for I had been afraid of a jealous scene and of what might occur if

Barron arrived unexpectedly, with Frank still in the flat. It would be necessary now for us to keep Barron's friendship, should we need his car to take Frank to Liverpool, and only Barron in the district would be able to supply us with false papers if Frank made a dash for Ireland. Not that from the start I had any faith in Frank's escaping the law, but I did not wish to express my sense of his folly when he was so obviously in need of a rest from prison routine. All that would result from his escape, I thought, would be my becoming implicated and charged for harbouring him. I saw that as inevitable and wished to postpone it for as long as possible.

I gave myself up to the delight of having him. He was completely mine. Part of his life had before been hidden with his mother; now all that was shared with me. He was in total reliance on me, and I was completely happy, though we lived behind drawn curtains. For want of anything to do, he did some housework while I was out—the first time in his life—and I looked after the cooking. I bought from a different butchers' for the double quantity of my purchases was so obvious.

Whenever I came back I stepped from the winter into warmth. Frank would be anxiously waiting for me, to read the papers, sometimes for food. At last I had one who waited for me to return; I wanted him never to go.

When I worked days, I guessed he slept, for he would be wakeful at night and sometimes I would wake to find him listening to gramophone records, especially old ones of Charlie Kunz. He staggered me by saying he had begun to learn to play the piano in prison. I had assumed from his not knowing how to write that he had never learnt anything there. When he mentioned Bach I wondered aloud.

"I'm not a dumb cluck," he protested indignantly. "What's the use of writing, anyway?"

"You could have sent me a letter."

"They read 'em," was his answer.

"You'll have to change your name to Murphy," said I. Frank was outlining his plan, not for the first time, of entering Ireland and Working there.

"Will you come too?"

"I don't expect there'll be much work for me," I commented gloomily. The prospect of Ireland chilled me. I had already pointed out that Ireland exported labourers and was not likely to be in much need of Frank's services. "I wish you spoke French," I said, with an envious side glance at Paris, "or Dutch even." It would be pleasanter to live in Paris or Amsterdam.

"What about Brazil?" Frank brightly suggested.

I considered it. Then my hopes fell. "How do we get I there?" I demanded. "Can you get to Brazil from Liverpool without a passport?"

"There's other ports," he said impatiently.

"They always get brought back, those who escape to South America."

"Christ!" he snorted. "They won't be looking all over South America, just for me—I'm not Eichmann. They'll forget about me in a bit."

"Then there's the fare."

"I could work my way."

"Sailors have unions."

"Aw hell," said he.

"If you could get to Ireland it might be easier for us to reach South America from there. We could work in a ship's kitchen perhaps." I felt almost persuaded of this, as so often when we made plans in the warmth of bed.

"You'd be a godsend to the crew," he said fondly, stroking me.

"I don't want to be sleeping with a lot of Irishmen."

"If one of the officers took a fancy to you, we'd have a whacky time of it," he meditated seriously, and I was reminded that he had served at sea. "Queers always get the best berths. It's bloody unfair."

But I knew Frank. Escaping the country needed organisation and work of a sort, so the days dreamily slipped by. Though I had, of course, known from the beginning, it was only gradually that I came truly to appreciate that I was sheltering an escaped convict. We could not go on for years living behind drawn curtains. If nobody else did, Miss Bee, the indefatigably inquisitive, would discover in time that there was a man hiding in the flat above. I began to worry and think we must do more than make vague plans for reaching Ireland. But a concrete course of action would mean confiding in Les Barron, and I hesitated to push Frank into a situation where he would be at Les' mercy. Frank procrastinated because he was comfortable, and I, because I did not want to change our enchanted world of two.

To my knowledge, Frank's presence with me was a secret from all in Hawkward. I had a tremendous shock when one afternoon at work, Milton came in and curtly informed me that a police officer was waiting to see me. I went dizzy and my heart seemed to jump into my head. It was a wonder I did not drop dead at once. In imagination one accepts arrest with some calm and dignity, but such was my timid and fearful nature I went into a paroxysm of nervous terror at once, blind and with trembling hands. There was a black bar, though, the back of my brain. When I came to, a red-faced bobby whom I recognised as Hurley was standing in front of me. There flashed through my brain the determination that even if I were crucified by them I would never give utterance to an incriminating word. My body was cowardly, but in spirit I knew I was stronger than the unjust law. I thought I was being interviewed as Frank's boy-friend, rather than as his known harbourer.

"Has there been an accident?" I managed to say, getting my word in first.

"I'm sorry to upset you, sir," said Hurley and I knew from the 'sir' that he had not recognised me as Frank's companion at the dance and elsewhere, "but Mr. Barraclough says you often work here at night and I was wondering if you might have some memory of a car that's been opposite your back gates nearly every night for a fortnight?"

It was some trivial parking affair, a dispute between neighbouring shopkeepers.

I did not tell Frank of the scare I had had, but from then on, I was sharply aware of the danger we were running.

As I came out of the off-licence, Les Barron barred my way. There was another man with him. I cursed Frank; he had been thirsting for beer and it was only for him that I had come out.

"Why have you been avoiding us?" asked Barron. "You've not been in the Whistle for over a month."

"There's a reason," I said slowly.

"I bet. You've become a secret drinker?"

"I've been busy."

I looked at Les' face—he did not seem exactly friendly. His companion was a slim dark young man whom I had seen dancing the twist at the Whistle. There was a sort of half-smile on his brown oval-shaped face; I couldn't make out whether he was sneering or amused or threatening.

"I've got to go to work," I lied. "But couldn't I see you at your place for a bit?" I thought that if I could separate Les from his companion it would be easier to make explanations. We were not far from Les' house. I had no intention of mentioning Frank before a witness.

"Come with us to the Whistle," said Les. "We've a bit of work ourselves, haven't we, Don?" His companion looked amused.

"Only for half-an-hour," I said.

"Look, Don," Les spoke with hurried urgency to his friend and there was that gleam about him which told me he now was eager to go with me. "I'll follow you on to the Whistle. Do you mind?"

"You want to keep your mind on the job," said Don sulkily.

"I won't be more than five minutes."

"In and out," said Don.

"See you, then."

With the bottles clanking in my pockets I was hurried by Les' side over the dark bridge to his house. He opened the front door and did not turn on the lights. He had me with brief brutality on the sofa. In such a hurried encounter hardly anything was said—certainly I couldn't tell him about Frank. Then after a hug he locked the front door and on the other side of the bridge went to join Don at the Whistle, while I departed "to work".

"You can get your own beer in future," I told Frank pettishly.

"How did I know you'd meet him? And don't say you didn't like it."

"Well, I didn't. I was only trying to be tactful. I couldn't say anything in front of his friend—Don, he called him."

"Oh, Don's all right," said Frank comfortably. "He's done time."

"What for?"

"Whipping cars. Did you see his knife?"

"Knife?"

"Well, it's more a glass cutter, for car windows. He's a good kid. A bit small for a real fist-fight if he's up against it. There's a lot of these gangs in London now. You haven't a chance. But he can meet six of them with his knife. It just dazzles in his hand."

My face showed what I thought.

"Oh he wouldn't have hurt you," said Frank in reassurance. "I bet he had his eye on you, come to that. He married when he was seventeen but he left her after six months. He was probably too shy to ask."

"Well, I'm not going out at night for any more bottles of beer. It's too risky—I'll see if I can't get some canned beer somewhere, in the daytime."

I stopped reading out of the newspaper. It was a couple of days later.

"Well go on, mutt," said Frank impatiently.

"Who's a mutt?" I said mechanically. "Frank, something's happened."

"What? Is it about me?" He was on his feet behind me looking to see if there was a photograph of himself. I pointed to a small paragraph.

"It's Les Barron. He's been arrested."

Frank sat down, disappointed. "What for?"

"Remanded in custody in connection with the disappearance of a car from Bramley Garages last Saturday....That was when I got you the beer."

Frank was profane. "It's not the first mucking car he's lifted. Have they got Don Meadows too?"

I read the piece again. "It says investigations are proceeding. What's Don Meadows to do with it?"

"What do you think he's in the district for? He must have blown in time." Frank laughed. "It's a long time since Les had porridge for breakfast. He'll get three years, I shouldn't wonder."

"I thought he was your friend."

Frank shrugged. I should have known better than to think criminals were ever true friends. We would probably all meet inside prison, I was thinking, and Les and Frank would behave like loving buddies. "You'll be able to go out for beer again without dropping your pants," said Frank cheerfully.

"Hmm." But bang went our only hope, I thought, of someone to help Frank out of the district, the country and recapture.

CHAPTER THIRTEEN

In the next week I was full of anxiety, nervously alert to sounds of people near the flat and suspicious of questions asked in the shops. Frank, too, seemed now more aware of his position. He went through more cigarettes than ever. He was careful, I noticed, not to play the gramophone when I was out of the flat. He seemed to be thinking a lot. He was also more considerate and loving, and told me more than once not to keep worrying.

"I'll never split on you, Johnny," he told me.

"But if they find you here?"

"I'll say I broke in. What's there to prove different?"

Tacitly we had come to see that we would not leave the country together except by a miracle. He was also very restless. I suppose that when he was alone, the flat, when he could not go out, was as much the same as prison. I could not rouse him from his brooding.

He was in this morose and thoughtful mood when we went to bed. It had been snowing all day, and I had to get up early the next morning for work by eight. I fell asleep exhausted. When I awoke there was a dim darkness still at the edge of the curtains, and a deep silence everywhere. I knew that he was awake. We lay in our drowsy lagoon of blankets, hearing the cold. The flow of his body was beside me, the earth seemed to have joined in our peace. His arm was about me, without passion, gently, protectingly. The moment was like that first morning when I awoke with him, yet still novel and uniquely fresh, as the hushed morning of Christmas Day is to a child. Only it was winter now and I was more aware of the cold outside our love.

"I'll always need you," Frank said. "Whatever happens, don't you go getting ideas I don't." He said no more. There was no need to. Words were always less than the implication of his warm presence.

It froze all that day. There was more than one collision between lorries on the icy main road through Hawkward and traffic was held up for hours. Extra police were called in from Pilney.

Though it was a comfortless day, it was warm enough inside Barraclough's because of the hatcheries, and in addition it was pay-day. Since we could not go out to celebrate I planned to bring back something specially delicious for our evening meal. I wanted to celebrate Frank's tenderness to me that morning. I felt it had been especial.

On my way back, a long procession of traffic at a standstill in the main road and the pavements slippery with ice, I shopped lavishly. I knew he had been craving for a joint, which I never bought whilst on my own, so I went out of my way to buy the best for him.

I arrived back frozen. The snow had not been cleared in the garden, except by Miss Bee's door, and it had now frozen hard. The string of the packages cut into my numbed hands. I put my key in the door and entered darkness. I wondered if he had fallen asleep with the lights off, but though I sought in every room he was nowhere. There was a terrible silence to the night, not a sound in the flat. I felt myself hurled into loneliness again, like a suicide in a winter river. I hadn't the heart to open the packages on the table.

The sequel came a few days later when I saw in the county's morning newspaper a small paragraph headed prisoner re-taken. No name was given but Frank was the only one who had recently escaped from that gaol. He had been re-captured in a large inland town many miles from Hawkward. I wondered about this. It seemed he had not been headed anywhere except away from Hawkward. The only explanation which I guessed at was, that appreciating he would be re-taken sooner or later, he had deliberately made it happen in a place as far away from me as possible so that I might not be charged with harbouring a fugitive.

CHAPTER FOURTEEN

It would have seemed that everything was how as it was before, but Les Barron was in prison, too, and this time I returned to lingering at the Whistle of my own free will, without inducement from Alf. Intimacy with Frank had spoilt me for loneliness that I had accepted with fair ease throughout my earlier life. But how as an escape from my own thoughts I wanted companionship, and at the Whistle there were companions. It was friendship, not love or sex, that I sought. I was too much under the spell of my affair with Frank, and too dazed, even to think of a new lover. Chatting with Alf and the men at the bar was pleasure enough for me. But if I had been sensible enough to know my own deeper motives, I would have understood that my need for male society was only half innocent. I had a sense of comfort being in proximity to their maleness and beautiful wild vigour. But it seemed innocent enough to drop in for a few drinks on those evenings when I was not working.

Don Meadows, whom I had met in Barron's company, was usually at the Whistle on Saturdays. He rather fancied himself as a crooner, and indeed did have a good voice, and would sing a few songs in the intervals of the juke-box. For all his imprisonment for car theft, odd though it sounds, the impression he gave me was of honesty. Crime had just been his metier. At present he was in a job and having a love affair with a sixteen-year-old girl, whom he could not marry as he was paying heavy weekly maintenance to his wife and child. He never brought the girl into the Whistle as she was under age, but met her in the market place at closing time. With being in Don's company I came to know many of the blue-jeaned angel-like youths in the heavy jackets more closely. Since I could play no card games, they taught me to play poker for matchsticks and, amid the repartee and talk of motor-bikes, I would sometimes have a couple of hours in the games-room at a game of cards.

If I were free on a Saturday or Sunday I began again, after a long lapse, to call upon my parents. I would ring them up before I set out, as their house was so isolated and in the snowy depths of winter they were quite likely to be in need of something from the shops on the way. In the winter my father's health was worse. The kitchen was always warm and cosy for at the weekend Jessie spent much of her time baking. In the sitting-room my father would be comfortably tucked in the armchair watching television. From the kitchen we could hear the rise and fall of the sports commentator's voice. Jessie was tempted to take her holidays in Italy, but was reluctant to go alone. My mother would have liked to go with her but was worried about leaving my father on his own. Discussing a holiday in Italy in the month of June was all the more delightful when the windows were blocked with snow and outside the trees rose blank and bare. As the 'plane and hotel reservations had to be made early, we decided to make bookings for two, then if circumstance allowed, my mother would go, and if not, I would accompany Jessie instead.

June seemed a long way off and I was not sure that I could persuade Milton to allow me my holidays in that month. But I had never been to Italy and the possibility of going there for the first time was exciting. There was too, the unspoken feeling on my part, that I would be in a freer world. I had no presentiment of what would happen before June. It seemed sad that Jessie could not go to Italy at the side of the man she loved, but this feeling was unspoken too, by both my mother and myself. I had guessed by pauses at some turns in the conversation that my mother knew Jessie's secret; the two had probably spoken together of it. But I kept mine still.

We had had school visits and occasional tours of our premises by overseas visitors in the past. Since the installation of Sara and the publicity given to Barraclough's as the most go-ahead poultry firm in the country, these visits had become more numerous. Now our fame was to be complete; a party of Japanese from a large company in

Japan were to spend a few days observing our methods, and one of the group was to remain with us for three months, his special interest being the sexing methods at Barraclough's. Milton enjoyed personally escorting important guests around the works and making speeches at the functions usually attendant on such visits. The Rotarians and business-men's organisations in the area were alerted and Milton prepared a few speeches stressing the resumption of Anglo-Japanese unity and the bond that existed between us in 1914. There were a few dissentients in our midst for some of the men had had relatives in Japanese hands during the last war, and others blamed Japanese competition for the decline in Lancashire. But the rest of us were rather in the dark. All the correspondence was on a thin tissue paper that floated into the air whenever the door was opened, and the typist seemed to have made many mistakes. I myself had never seen a Japanese, except in the numerous war films made after the war, but we had all heard that the Japanese poultry-sexers were virtually clairvoyant. Bill Gates swore they could tell the sex of a fertilised egg by holding a gold ring on a thread over it, and the Chinese used this method (said he) to determine the sex of an unborn child. Gates had been a prisoner in the Far East (he said he would turn his back if any of the Japs spoke to him; he'd never eaten a rice pudding since he was freed) and we thought the Japanese sexer, an old man swinging a gold ring, would be overwhelmed when he came by our scientific statistical approach and electrical equipment. My part in the business was to find accommodation for the sexer. Milton was seeing to all the wining and dining of the big-wigs (who were to stay at Hawkward's best inn). He told the inn's manager by 'phone that no expense was to be spared in securing sake from London. After all, he told the directors, we had captured the Italian market and who knew but that before long in this scientific age we would be despatching processed chicken or eggs for incubation to Japan at rates below the Americans?

The Japanese were a quiet, smiling, heavily spectacled lot, all dressed like cabinet ministers in impeccable suits and making a great fuss about Milton going first through the doorways. They spoke with heavy American accents and had more precise technical information about the equipment than Milton himself. One was six-foot tall, and looking for the yellow we found instead a light bronze brown, as if they had just had a week on the Riviera.

The sexer's name was Nobuyuki Takahara, which I had earlier memorised by writing on my wrist and consulting till it was stamped on my memory. He was in his early twenties and slender, so that he looked even younger, and he had a degree in science. He had rich black hair and an oval Caucasian face. His teeth were much admired by the office girls and within a week he was escorting them to the cinemas and the coffee-shops in Hurley. I had located a furnished flat in the centre of Hawkward—a rather charming one looking onto the river and the old bridge—and he seemed to settle down well. He did not drink, but on my comings and goings to the Whistle I could see whether he had returned by the lights from his flat shining in the water.

CHAPTER FIFTEEN

I was working at Christmas but I spent New Year's Eve with my parents. None of the family were dark and there was no near neighbour whom we could ask to be a first-footer, I had therefore asked Mr. Takahara to accompany me and bring in the luck of the house. No head of hair could be darker than his and we might well hope for a greater largesse of luck in the coming year, though perhaps it would be of a Japanese variety. Takahara enjoyed himself. He got on very well with Jessie and told her how to make o-mochi, the Japanese rice-cake eaten at the New Year. A few minutes before midnight he was locked outside with the lump of coal and piece of bread in his hand. Then, as the solemn strokes of Big Ben trembled inside the house and the bells from the churches in Hawkward and the neighbouring villages sounded more faintly in the valley, he was let in to receive wine and our greetings.

At half-past twelve we left. I would have liked to stay longer but I had to be at the hatchery by eight in the morning. It was Sunday and I would virtually be in charge. Milton had asked me (almost apologetically, for him) to work this Sunday, which would normally have been my free one, as the pressure of work made my presence indispensable. I had previously booked a taxi and as Takahara and I rode home together I felt peacefully tired. But for work in the morning I would have asked him to my flat to bring in the luck and carry the festivities further. We had had a pleasant evening and I had enjoyed his company. I had been surprised to learn that his father was the head of the firm in Japan and that as the eldest son he was learning all sides of the business in the English way by working his way up. After dropping Takahara, the taxi took me on to the flat. I paid up and the taxi-driver departed. I entered the garden, turning on my torch.

Some snow as fine as sugar was thinly falling. I thought I saw a dark figure slip around the side of the house, but all was quiet. It must have been the shadow of a tree. Reassured, I turned the key in the door.

Then they were all upon me, rushing from the gloom and pushing me inside. My heart sank in utter dismay. At first I did not know what was happening. There were six of them, strapping young men in age ranging from twenty to thirty, all of whom I had seen at some time or other at the Pole and Whistle, though I knew none of them well. One of them, in the blue jeans and a Hawaian shirt, had been pointed out to me as a dangerous type who had served a three years prison sentence for violent assault. They were all drunk, very drunk, leering and grinning at me.

"We thought you'd be lonely. 'Let's go up to Johnny's and have some fun,' Tony said. We've brought our own supper," one of them said.

"Look!" cried another, producing sausages.

"We haven't come to eat off you," the eldest of them, a big sunburnt fellow, explained.

"No, we've come to give," said another in double-entendre. The man in the Hawaian shirt was rapping at Miss Bee's window, which was in darkness. I hoped that she was out.

"What's he doing?" I protested.

"He's after the dame in there. She came out before."

"She's over sixty," I said.

"Hey, Beggy, Johnny says she's over sixty."

"Get him away from the window," I begged the big man. "She'll call the police." But he only grinned drunkenly. I realised that I could not appeal rationally to any of them. Already upstairs in the flat I could hear noises of pans dropping and things being moved. The big man had his arm about me. "You'll let us kip here for the night, won't you, Johnny? We've nowhere to go."

I made no reply. When I thought of the work waiting for me in the morning I felt desperate. I was about to appeal again for the man called Beggy to come away from the window when he came of his own accord, locking and bolting the downstairs entrance to the flat. I was now imprisoned with the six of them. I could only hope they would sober up in time. Perhaps by two or three o'clock they would leave, and I could snatch a little sleep before leaving for work. In the kitchen they were drunkenly trying to fry the sausages— the crash of dishes and the drunken roars of laughter filled the flat. Beggy was roaming around looking at letters, opening drawers and pocketing ties. I was glad there was no money in the flat. He turned the radio on, locating a continental station.

"Where's Uncle Fred, the old, old bed?" asked the big sunburnt man. "You can bring our meal to us. Don't look so miserable, Johnny. It's not kind. Frank Jeffers said you liked a big one. Isn't this big enough?"

He had his arm crooked about my throat as if to crush my neck and had pushed me into the bedroom. His voice was angry because I showed no enthusiasm.

"Shall I hold him for you?" asked Beggy, who had stopped his exploration and followed in lascivious expectation of what might follow.

It ran through my mind that by reaching the telephone I could summon the police. But nothing that could now happen, even my murder, would be worse than the shock to my family of a scandal involving the police. These men would, of course, lie and in their revenge would probably implicate Frank. By suffering whatever I had to suffer, I could at least confine the disaster to myself. Love-making without tenderness is a degradation but it was soon apparent that I was to undergo worse than this. The man called Beggy was a sadist. The straightforward satisfaction of his lust would have been harmless compared with his delight in inflicting pain. It began with his stabbing lighted cigarettes on my naked flesh then scattering boiling oil from the frying pan. He stopped only because some of the oil went on his companions while they were involved with me. I had gradually become insensible.

Later, I found myself in a chair in the living-room with someone holding a cup of tea to my lips. The man in the Hawaian shirt was standing up and talking, his eyes glittering. The others were slumped in chairs, quiet, as if they were sobering up. The radio was silent, the continental programme ended at three in the morning. I wished they would go.

They sat as if waiting. Now and then one of them would speak, jocularly, but it was mainly Beggy who did the speaking. I could see the others were afraid of him. I was afraid of him myself. He seemed to me insane.

"Why doesn't he speak?" he suddenly spat out, wheeling on me in anger.

There was complete silence from everybody.

"This punk's just waiting for us to go so he can call the cops."

"No, I'm not," I said faintly.

"Don't you answer me, you bloody pervert," said Beggy. "What's Frank Jeffers got that he's welcome and we're not? He used to joke about you. It was only that he could scrounge a meal or a few bob out of you."

"I don't believe you," I said, but I did.

Beggy threw the table over with a crash. "I'm going to kill you," he said. Everyone sat mute. The big brown-faced man leaned back and closed his eyes. Beggy advanced and crashed his fist in my face. He did this repeatedly and I felt the blood liquid on my face and in my mouth. I could not see.

"He's only a girl, Beg," someone dared to say, as if in frightened remonstrance. The voice seemed a long way off. I lost consciousness.

When I came to I was very cold. Beggy was kneeling before me, blubbering. "Say you'll forgive me, Johnny. I don't know what I do when I've had some drinks. I can't help myself. I know I'm a nut-case. I'm only like that when I'm drunk. That's why I got into trouble every time."

I said nothing, for I could say nothing. The blood had dried and glued my lips. I would never forgive him. I would never forgive any of them.

"Say you won't go to the cops."

I nodded. They talked among themselves. I was too filled with nausea and the beginnings of pain to notice what they were doing, but I heard them descending the stairs.

The brown faced man had remained behind the others.

"I'm sorry, kid," he muttered in a low voice. "You were lucky Beggy didn't chiv you or put the boot in. He's a sod when drunk. He'd have killed us if we'd tried to stop him— we shouldn't have come."

The others called for him. He hastened away. I do not know how long it was before I stirred. I groped my way to the kitchen for hot water. It took courage to look at my face. The left eye was closed and I could see nothing with it. The right side of my mouth was split an inch-and-a-half into the cheek. When I removed the dry blood, fresh blood welled forth. I was distantly aware of burns and scalds all over my body. It was now six o'clock, but I had not been conscious for part of the time and it had not seemed so long a time to me. By degrees I was becoming aware of vague centres of pain throbbing where I had known nothing to occur. With the split at the side of my mouth I could not eat, but I drank hot tea and swallowed what aspirins there were in the house. All my endeavour was to remain conscious and capable of the day's work. At least Milton would not be at the works to see me and enquire what had happened. I could scarcely tell anyone I had walked into a door, and I could not disguise my disfigurements. I tried to plaster the side of my mouth in an attempt to stop the bleeding. My main concern was that people should not see me as it would be difficult to explain away such injuries. For me personally, the true injury was not in the blows or the cruelty or the degradation, but in Beggy's crude statement that Frank had not loved me for myself, that in all probability he had talked and joked about me with those hooligans, that it had all been deceit on his part.

Every despair is different; words are blunt to convey the infinite shades of grief. If I had once been in the dreariness of despair because I could never realise my love, my heart was now stone, because I had learnt that love had been an imposture and had not existed. Every trust in me was petrified. I was aware that morning, as I waited for the light to come in the sky, when I could summon a taxi to take me to work, that I would never trust a human being again. It was the bitterest knowledge; the world was empty of affection. I wanted just to get through the work and the day as I had promised Milton. Beyond that I had no feeling and no hope.

The taxi-driver gave me a quick startled look. As I paid him off at the gates, a policeman came past, staring intently, then grinning slightly. I expect he thought I had been in a domestic row, a rather violent one. I was thankful that I could work quietly in the office, with most of the staff away, and push matters through over the telephones. It was nearly eleven before I was disturbed and then only by Takahara. I kept my face averted from him as much as possible. The split mouth must have made my voice different. He came round the desk to look at me.

"What has happened to you?"

"I was beaten up."

"But when?"

"Last night. After I left you."

"It is very bad. Have you told the police?"

"No."

"In Japan we would tell the police when a gang attacks." I was silent. "Is it a very powerful gang?"

"No, it's not that. I can't go to the police. They would say I was the criminal."

"I do not understand."

We were alone. He looked sympathetic. I felt wretched. For the first time in my life I told the truth about myself to another. He listened in silence, surprised.

"It would not be so in Japan," he observed. "The bad men would not be allowed to do what they have done to you."

"The law is different in England," I said dryly.

"You would be happier to live in Japan."

"I wish I could," I said bitterly.

"It would not be difficult to arrange. Our firm has much correspondence in English, and you know the business. Would you want to go if I asked my father?"

"Yes, of course."

"You would have to learn Japanese."

In my reaction from the occurrences of the night before I would have agreed to go anywhere. With the throbbing of physical pain I was wandering in remote places of consciousness and what I said did not seem to me like a decision. Seeing me wince Takahara insisted, when I rejected his advice to see a doctor at once, that at least he should fetch some of the first-aid supplies from another floor and help me patch up my face. The antiseptic cream was infinitely cool.

Somehow or other the day was got through and at last came to a close. I was beginning to lose consciousness and I did not refuse when Takahara offered to take me home. The flat was in the mess it had been left that morning. He saw me to bed and, I believe, tidied up the main rooms, for the disarray seemed less when I opened my eye to find he had summoned a doctor. The side of my mouth was stitched together and I was given a sedative. With relief I fled from consciousness.

CHAPTER SIXTEEN

I awoke to the telephone's ringing. It was Takahara, who had apparently stayed till late at the flat and now wished to explain what disposition he had made about food and so on and what explanation he had given the firm about my absence. After twenty hours' sleep I was more in a condition to appreciate his kindness. The doctor was going to give a certificate of sickness and all was smooth and orderly with the firm. I had a little hot soup in the kitchen and thankfully crept back to bed.

The next time I woke it was to the sound of a car, steps on the stairs and a buzz on the bell. I had a dismayed feeling it was the police. Looking out of the window I could see the pink bonnet of a car. Whoever it was, it could not be the police. I opened to Don Meadows.

He was in a very smart suit, his shoes pointed.

"God, you haven't half had it!" he exclaimed.

"Is it your car?" I asked with the unmistakable implication that it might be stolen.

He grinned and followed me in. "Yes—at least it's Tom Richards'. He's trying to sell it. If I'd whipped it, it wouldn't be that colour."

"If you'd like some tea, could you make it? I'd like some myself."

"Right-o. You look as if you'd walked into a bus."

"I wish I had. I wouldn't be surprised if I never see again with this."

"Did he put the boot in?"

"No."

"Well, you were lucky. That Beggy's a bloody menace. I heard about it last night. They're scared stiff you'll go to the police. You've got them where you want them, Johnny."

"The police? How can I? That Beggy went down on his knees and asked me not to tell on him. But he knew I couldn't."

"Why not? You could be Mr. X."

"There's Frank and Les."

"They'd split on you if you were down. Did they steal anything?"

"I suppose Beggy did. He was looking everywhere."

"There you are. Robbery with violence. The police would give anything to get him inside."

"It would be easier for me to leave the country," I said wearily.

"Where to ?" he asked with interest.

"Oh—Paris," I lied. I was not going to reveal my true plans.

"Well, if I were in your place I'd split on the lot of them. They're dead scared expecting you to. I think they want to come and say they're sorry."

"A fat lot of good that is," I said bitterly. "It was New Year's Eve and I hadn't asked any of them to come here."

"They're a dangerous lot. Especially that Beggy. They wouldn't have come if Frank had been around."

"They were drunk," I said in mitigation.

"That's when Beggy goes wild. He said they didn't come with any wrong intentions but when you didn't seem very welcoming they saw red."

"It's not much comfort now. And however tough they are, six to one isn't fair. Not that I could have managed one even."

"It's a rough place, the Whistle. Not that I've any time for types like Beggy," said Don seriously as he helped himself to sugar. "You never hear a squeak out of him in stir. The fellows would paste him one. Most of them are tougher than him."

"What's that?" I asked Don as he felt in the pocket of his overcoat and produced a parcel. He opened it.

"It's a truncheon."

"What for?"

"You're worse than a woman," he said with mild but friendly exasperation. "To dot them one, of course. Anyone coming here has to round the top of the stairs. That's when you will crack them with

93

this truncheon. Here, just bring it down like this. You could keep an army out if you hold the top of the stairs with a truncheon."

"You might split somebody's skull," I commented.

"They split your mouth, didn't they, not to mention....Or do you want them to do it again?"

"Of course not. But they aren't likely to come again."

Don looked at me as a professor regards his worst pupil. "You haven't been around much, Johnny, have you? You're not going to the cops and so nothing will happen. But Beggy will get drunk again— either a Friday or a Saturday night. You can expect to see that lot again."

I sat mute with dismay.

"You use that truncheon. And don't just wave it as though you were conducting Beethoven or that old corn. Wham it down!" He eyed me appraisingly. "I don't know how you've kept alive. You couldn't knock the skin off a rice pudding. If you want me to, I'll come and keep guard on a Friday and Saturday night. After closing time. That's the time for danger. Beggy would know better than to take me on, and I'd knife the bugger if he did."

He seemed to read my thoughts. "I'm not wanting anything out of it. I just don't want to see you thrown to the wolves, and Les would like me to keep an eye on you. He was a good pal to me. You'd be safe with me."

He sounded reassuring. I accepted his offer of protection.

"There's no insurance on the car, so I'd better not leave it out there too long," said Don easily.

"I might have known there was something wrong with it," I said.

"You worry too much," Don. said, going. "See you Friday."

The buzzer rang again, timidly this time. It could not be Don as I had seen the car drive away. Takahara was at the hatcheries. Expecting a surprise I opened the door and was more surprised than I had dreamt. It was my mother.

Her cheeks were bright with cold, her eyes were bright also, but not with cold.

"Are the police gone?" she asked in a low urgent voice.

"Police?" I echoed.

"I came about an hour ago but I saw the car outside, so I walked down to the bus-shelter and stayed there."

"No, that was a friend. The police don't have pink Zephyrs, mother. Come to the fire, and take your coat off."

I thought Takahara or Milton must have telephoned her, and I did not thank them for their intervention. My mother took her hat and coat off and sat down to one side of the electric fire. I sat opposite her on the other.

"I came," said my mother simply, "as soon as I heard you were in trouble through being a homosexual. When I saw the car I naturally thought it was the police."

I was too surprised to say anything. There had been nothing of exclusion in my mother's tone; I was still her son. I had been afraid for so many years of the shock to her if she knew, and now that she knew the shock was mine.

"After I left you on New Year's night I came straight back here and found six drunks. They more or less forced their way in and when I asked them to go they became nasty. They were drunk. I didn't tell the police."

"I thought you couldn't have asked them. It was so late when you left us. You had such beautiful eyes, John," she said with attention to my face. "It's poor Jessie I'm worrying about. She has always admired you so much. It will be a shock to her."

"I don't think you need worry about Jessie, mother." I thought of the unspoken things between my sister and myself. "She is less of a child than you think. And she will always have known how different I was to the other men, vaguely known, but now she will know clearly. It is you I never expected to understand. I never wanted you to know."

"I knew. Only, you had so much control I thought it would be for ever."

After a while I said, "It is better to be dead than live without love. The love of a man," I added, to be clear. I did not want to hurt her by implying I had not known the more lasting love.

95

She sighed. We sat silent.

"I don't think it was my fault," she said at last, more to herself it seemed.

"No, of course not. Perhaps, sometimes, I've thought my father should have given me a more robust personality as a pattern in my childhood. But I know that isn't the truth. A less gentle father would have been more disastrous. I was born the way I am. Only I am to blame. It was the same from the start. You are the one who will suffer because you had such hopes for me and pride in me. I suffer less because at last I have come to accept myself as l am."

"I accept you as you are," said my mother.

"I'll make some tea," I said.

There is a turmoil and tranquillity when at last our inmost secret is wrested from us. I stood stunned before the depths of my mother's love. Of a conventional nature, she could put aside the judgments of convention for my sake. I had found for my maturer years an enduring friend.

It was not until we were having the tea that I thought to check on my mother's sources of information. She told me she had heard from Mrs. Cartwright.

"Mrs. Cartwright?" I was mystified as it was years since I had spoken to this chubby little woman who lived in the road leading to the village nearest my parents.

"Yes, Mrs. Cartwright. She had heard it all from Mrs. Wain, who knows Miss Bee in the local history group. Miss Bee had said she was so upset that she felt forced to go to the police. She had seen a terrible face at her window on New Year's night, and she could not endure all the men coming to your flat."

"There was only one, mother," I said. "Till that night."

"Well, Miss Bee puts it at hundreds, and she says she has watched you in her mirror bringing back crates of beer, night after night."

I thought of the few bottles I had brought back for Frank.

"Miss Bee certainly has made me an item of local history," I remarked.

"And Mrs. Dempster who keeps the woollen shop had told Mrs. Cartwright that you were badly hurt, and all about New Year's night."

"Mrs. Dempster—is she in the local history brigade too?"

"Her husband has a taxi."

"Ah yes." I recollected that Dempster was the taxi-driver I had summoned on January the first.

"At the rate Miss Bee travels—after all, she is a member of everything that one could be a member of—the whole of Hawkward will know about you."

"And have it wrong—I would have thought there would have been enough without inventing crates of beer."

"My worry is whether she has been to the police or not."

"They have not been here—yet," I said. "I could scarcely be arrested because someone else looked in her window. But I would not want the attention of the police directed to me at all. I need the kindly shadows."

"Things cannot go on as they are," my mother said.

"There is a possibility," I said slowly, "that I could go to Japan."

I saw the dread and dismay in my mother's face.

"It would not be for ever. You would have Jessie, mother."

"Aren't you happy at Barraclough's?" she asked inconsequentially.

"The hours are very difficult, these topsy-turvy nights and days, nothing regular; I would not have chosen to live in England, alone." I thought of Frank. "Even for your sakes, it would be better now for me not to stay. I would be a foreigner there, and perhaps I am meant always to live as a foreigner. Nobuyuki is asking his father. Nothing may come of it. It is only a possibility."

My mother's face softened with relief. "You cannot stay alone here, in the state you are in. You had better come to us. It is your home."

"No, I can manage. If there is trouble with the police it is better to have this address publicised. My family must be involved as little as possible. It would be difficult enough for you all in any case."

"While I'm here, I'll tidy the place, though it looks better I than I expected, I must say. I'd stay longer but your father will be wondering where I've got to."

"Nobuyuki cleaned up."

"He has been a true friend to you. Is he——?"

"No, only a friend."

I had begun to tremble with pain.

"You had better go back to bed. Have you eaten?"

I took her advice. Again I had some hot soup, for it was difficult to move my mouth for solid food. When finally I | heard the outer door close behind my mother, I was already half-asleep, feeling a sort of empty exhausted tranquillity. I had been accepted for what I was by three people. I was without the tension of a secret. I was without the looming dread of injuring my mother, for the worst had happened, her knowledge, and she was wiser and more tacitly sympathetic than I had dreamed. I was also without the feeling of closeness to and rest in another, for Frank had fallen out of my life.

In my inrushing sleep there came the image of a black torii standing half-sunk in a dark sea with a greyly darkened sky behind. I had seen in my childhood a plate with such a Japanese design. The plate had belonged to my grandmother. But in my dream this torii or ceremonial temple gateway seemed real, not a static representation. I heard the solemn rush of the waves. The sea swirled through the smooth pillars on the dark horizon, as sleep swirled and drowned me.

CHAPTER SEVENTEEN

As my body healed I saw that I would carry the scars for life. I would at least carry no scar in my mind for the friendly offices of Takahara and Don and the loyalty and unreproaching love of my mother had been timely; my bitterness had been outbalanced by their rallying to me. The discoloration was gradually fading from my eye, but it was becoming apparent that the sight might be destroyed or at the best severely impaired. The doctor urged me to see a specialist at once, but this would have meant long journeys to a distant city and it was still winter. I intended to consult the specialist nearer the Spring. I was not without hope that the doctor was being too gloomy.

Don came every Friday and Saturday evening. He brought the gossip of the Pole and Whistle with him, and he came prepared to do battle. With him around it seemed I would have no need to use the truncheon myself. At the Whistle they knew nearly every move made at the police station and so Don was able to inform me that Miss Bee had not called there to complain; she was doing all the complaining at the local history circle and other groups to which she belonged.

After I had told Don about the injury to my eye he mentioned it to Alf Shaw and it came to the ears of Beggy and his friends.

"They're scared stiff," said Don with satisfaction. "They think you may be able to claim compensation from them."

"It's not possible," I said. "And if it were, none of them has much money."

"That's what they're frightened of—you awarded thousands and they in and out of stir for non-payment. I don't know why you're laughing."

"If I can't afford a glass-eye—if it comes to that—I'll think of taking Beggy to court."

While I was away from work, Takahara also called on me, but he and Don never encountered each other at the flat. I was unwilling that they should meet and thankful that they did not. I did not want Takahara to be involved in any way with the world of The Pole and Whistle. My conversations with Don, in which prison, the police, gangs and Don's lovelife played such a large part, would have given him an odd idea of England, and I felt he had already encountered a less peaceful aspect of it through me, without needing any more.

Nothing had changed at Barraclough's. Milton was the same to me as he had always been. No rumour had reached him. I had the same unpredictable style of work—nights and days irregularly mixed —and it was all the more fatiguing now that I was with the use of only one eye. I was never certain in advance of the free disposal of a day and this compelled me to put off making the appointment with the eye specialist. After being absent with a doctor's certificate I could not now ask for a full day off without giving Milton the explanation. The days and nights dragged along. I was exhausted with working long hours in the glare of the office electricity, and after a night of it I was glad of sleep's soothing darkness.

Then Takahara heard from Japan that it could be arranged for me to go there and I was shaken out of my torpor. It was necessary to have a visa and till that was forthcoming I thought it better not to inform Milton, and so asked Takahara not to mention anything. Takahara was leaving for Japan in early March and I would have liked to accompany him. I began to make my plans to that end. Some vaccinations would be necessary, and I would terminate the tenancy of the flat in March. Knowing the speed with which news spread about Hawkward, I spoke about my leaving to no one but my family. I wished my departure, when it came, to be unheralded and quiet.

At the flat I began to sort out and pack things away in readiness. Most things I would leave at my parents. The place began to look a little bare to me, but I don't think Don noticed when he came. March was approaching and there was still no sign of my visa. Milton had not been told. Without the visa I could not go with Takahara; I would have to make the journey later, alone. There was no particular haste for me to arrive in Japan, so I could go by sea. The ship would stop at different countries and I would have the rest and interest of a voyage, and save money too. Takahara said that while in London he would call at the Japanese Embassy and try to hasten up the visa.

I bought a Japanese grammar. I arranged to leave the flat early in March and, even though the visa had still not come, I finally gave a month's notice to Milton. He called my action 'foolhardy' and 'rash' and solemnly asked me to reconsider 'in my own best interests'. He reminded me more than ever of my old headmaster. I could not discuss the true reasons for my decision with him, and so our interview was unrealistic. He quite properly pointed out that I was not considering the welfare and interests of my future wife and children. My silence must have struck him as sullen and obstinate. He became angry and red. Doing so, he said he was not going to mention my gratitude or lack of it. My last month at Barraclough's was clearly going to be the worst.

"Mr. Anselm, I have always said you were the quiet, ideal neighbour." It was Miss Bee who, driven by curiosity as my small amount of furniture was taken out to the van, had appeared smiling with a parting present of a hydrangea cutting in a pot. "I don't know what I shall do without you. Really. I know that children must live somewhere but I cannot pretend that I would like them running about over my head. A single person is so much better. Well, I'm an old maid."

"I don't know who the new tenants will be."

"It really is a blow, your going. It has come as such a surprise."

"My father is not in very good health," I stated truthfully, but with a lying purpose. I was surprised myself that with departure I was to live in legend as the ideal neighbour.

"Your mother will be so glad to have you with her again, and to keep an eye on you," said Miss Bee either innocently or showing her claws. "It's such a cold morning, perhaps these two hard workers would like a cup of tea—or something stronger—before they go?"

I knew Miss Bee kept a bottle of whisky, strictly in the interests of gossip.

"It's kind of you, ma'am, but we've had one nip and I'm driving," one of them answered.

We squeezed into the cabin, the hydrangea on my knee. Miss Bee smilingly waved and through the glass asked to be remembered to my mother and sister. I replied with as sweet a smile.

"I'd say that one wanted a man," the driver remarked lightly, and the engine roared.

CHAPTER EIGHTEEN

The buds were opening on the beech trees and the tips of the pines were a new light green. I walked in the woods with my sister. The paths were all open, thick with beech leaves that had lain here all winter. Through the tall trunks and the boughs not yet obscured with leaves, the rounded lulls were seen, like smooth, firm limbs under the tender blue sky.

The leaves rustled under our feet.

"I'll send you a kimona," I said.

"I shouldn't worry too much about mother," said Jessie. "Once you're gone she'll accept it and settle down. But write often. She'll be happy talking about you."

"She didn't see much of me when I was in Hawkward."

"No, but she could have, and now she can't."

"If you can get her to Italy she will be happy enough. It will help to drive me out of her mind."

"She'll have to go now," said Jessie. "We can't give up two bookings, and she's keen on foreign countries now you're to be in one."

"I wish I could remember Japanese words more easily," I said, producing a scrap of paper. I carried lists about with me all the time. "They just dissolve in my mind."

"Oh it will come," Jessie comforted. "I wish I was going." I looked at her. "Life must be full of new things in a strange country. Well, Italy will be enough of a change for me."

"Let me find out what it's like first then you can come out to me."

"No, it's too far. It's better just to dream about," she said laughing, her wistfulness vanishing.

I knew I would often think back to this sky and the awakening woodlands with the gentle thrill of Hawkward Water, as at the same time I remembered the woods last Summer with Frank, now in prison, and his mother dead. My face showed the shadow.

"You will miss the woods," she said.

"Oh Jessie!" I recovered myself. "Takahara is there so it isn't as if there is nobody not a stranger."

"You're bound to be homesick and lonely at first."

"No, I'll never be homesick. I won't allow myself to. It would be too easy and destroying. I know I couldn't stop, so I'll never start."

There was only one cloud in the sky. Jessie watched it out of sight. "It will be cold tonight," she said.

"Shall we turn back?"

"No, let's see the valley-head. There's time."

We used to come here in childhood. The trees had thinned out and before us in a lonely bowl the banks of bracken and heather sloped steeply down to where Hawkward Water began at the junction of the two streams that were fed from the moors. There was a fallen sheepfold made of local stone; in its ruined state it resembled a circle of sun worship by the Britons who had survived here even after the Danes came. There was the cry of one curlew, like a sound in eternity.

I held my sister's hand. The sun stayed late in this upland nook, long after it had departed from Hawkward. We did not want to walk back through the dark woods, but there was a temple-realm in this sunny desolation. In a fold of the hills just beyond the valley-head was a tiny new unused chapel. Our ashes would rest there. Here were our gods.

My visa had come. I was now waiting for the shipping company to inform me of a vacancy on the next ship leaving for Japan.

"Shall we wait to see the sun set?" Jessie asked.

"If you like, but we'll have to go the long way home, by the road. We have no torch."

"I don't mind the walking—and someone may give us a lift."

As the sun descended, the bracken and withered heather on the folding hills became distinctly illuminated in the brilliant flood of golden light. Then as the sun reddened and distended, the hills became black bulks. Sky and earth were like flushing charcoal; Hawkward Water ran lurid. Jessie's face was delicately crimsoned. "Well, it should be the Rising Sun soon," she said as we hastened to the path that would lead to the road.

CHAPTER NINETEEN

My sister's employer, Harry, drove us to the docks. He had some business in the vicinity of the port and had kindly offered to transport my parents, myself and the luggage. Jessie came along too. It was a large car and even with us all there was comfort.

The long journey across country by minor roads gave me my last view of the English hills and fields. Though it was Spring, as we came into the congestion of towns, a fog closed about us. We had all risen about five o'clock and were whitefaced and uncommunicative, sinking into the comfort of the car as if it were a second bed. I think my father was actually asleep. I had slept only about half-an-hour the night before and now I was tense with anxiety not to say anything which could cause my mother upset. She was raw with emotion as if at my death-bed, but was keeping herself rigidly under control. Only Jessie was natural and vivacious, keeping her eyes on the road and helping Harry to negotiate the fog, which was becoming more and more difficult. He and she kept up a lively conversation about the bad posting of road signs in this part of England and about the difference the new road would make when it was built.

My mother sat silent. She was wearing a flowery little hat and a new green coat as if to emphasise the specialness of the occasion. My father had been forced into his best suit and a stiff new hat, looking unnatural, as if to provide the discomfort which shows especialness. I had every pocket full of tickets, visa, documents, money and sea-sick tablets and felt in a panic about ever finding any of them again when required. I had dressed with half an eye on the tropics, but seeing the coldness of the morning had put on a few woollens. Takahara had left me vague whether I was to be among palms or polar bears and I had prepared a little for each eventuality in my wardrobe but had mainly left the matter to be settled when I was in Japan.

We crept around the crumblingly dirty huge wall of a prison and I winced, feeling a numb relief that I was slipping past it to the sea and freedom, but with my mind swirling with a jumble of memories and thoughts of Frank. I smelt the sweetness of his hair, touched and knew his sculptured body, and I felt a helplessness of anger that for a stupid, little and unsuccessful crime he was in prison, leaving his mother to die alone and myself to look for kindness from men of another race.

We pulled up with a jerk. A roadside cafe, one that was open, had appeared in the fog. I had been told to appear for the customs examination at eleven, and having breakfasted so early, it seemed we might be late for a regular lunch. We were all glad of the hot cups of tea; the meal, greasy egg and bacon, seemed appropriate to the foggy weather. We got ready to go on our way again. I saw a pillar-box in the fog and posted a small package addressed to Don. There was a cornelian ring inside for him to give to Frank when he came out of prison. Frank could pawn or sell it. He was bound to be short of money.

As the docks drew near there was the sense of civilisation coming to an end: bare streets ending on nothing, vast empty buildings, silent driverless lorries, sheets of bare dirty water, and then the ships looming mysterious in the mist, the black and white marus from Japan, the Russian ship reeking of sunflower seeds, with the smell of salt, rotting rope and oil and the shriek of a seagull from the foggy river. We drove slowly, looking for a sign to the right dock. There seemed to be no living beings about. Then at last a great iron-covered shed and within, on the far side, my ship, looming with the gangway down.

Great sheets of trembling sheet-iron were being carried through the air by cranes, and trolleys piled with crates swerved past us wherever we stood. Men's voices carried and echoed under the vast metal roofing. The car was clearly in the way. It was an awkward place for leave-taking when one had to keep dodging out of the way of

107

trolleys. Harry had to go on to his business appointment and was already late because of the fog. My sister was to go with him. They made an arrangement to re-meet my parents in the early evening at a hotel. I shook hands with my sister, then Harry. It was a cheerful leave-taking. Jessie was in her prime of beauty. She was not unnoticed by the men working on the dock or looking from the ship's rails. It was not only a physical beauty, but a beauty in her nature, a quality of trust and innocence like a radiance. I wondered what her life would hold the next time I saw her again. With smiling eyes and lips she turned to leave. She gave a last wave from the car.

Our presence with my sister's had been noticed from the ship and two young stewards, looking in their teens and very shy, now came to take the luggage and ask us on board. We went up the gangway and I had just manipulated my parents on deck when a fussy looking little man with a moustache exclaimed sharply: "Are you all passengers? No. It's preposterous. Customs regulations cannot be flouted like this. Only passengers are allowed on board. I am surprised this should have occurred. It is most unauthorised, there's always a risk of stowaways."

"We'll stay below till the ship sails," I said stiffly. "Let's know."

We got down the gangway with its precarious rope balustrade. There were some sacks against one wall of the building and my father took a seat on these. My mother had to keep standing as the sacks were dirty.

"Well," said my father. "I don't know how he got the idea I wanted to be a stowaway to Japan."

One of the young stewards hurried down and across to us. "You don't want to pay any attention to that old crow, Mr. Anselm," he said in a strong local accent. "They give you the pip, Customs. We always have a bit of a barney with that one. He's like that."

I was concerned for my father. It was very cold and fog from the river was drifting into the big shed. The din was shattering with the clang of iron and the grind of trolleys on the concrete floor. After half-an-hour, the chief steward, fat-faced with round spectacles glinting, hurried across to us to say that he was trying to arrange for my parents to come aboard.

An hour elapsed. I suggested in vain that my parents should leave me and shelter in a warmer place. My mother was determined to see the ship leave. I asked a man passing on a trolley if there were any cocoa-rooms or anywhere to have a cup of tea on or near the dock, but he told me there was not. I went to investigate for myself but found only a desolation of sheds and empty roads seemingly endless.

An hour later, again the Customs official was with us, explaining that he thought we might be allowed to go on board and he would do all he could to obtain permission.

"What about the Customs' examination of my luggage?" I enquired.

He gave a startled little shrug. His new sweetness of manner I attributed to pressure put upon him by the chief steward.

Three hours after we had arrived at the dock we were allowed aboard and shown to the passengers' lounge where other passengers and their guests were having coffee under a portrait of the Queen. I was glad to see my parents at least seated, but lunch was over. The lounge steward offered coffee and while my parents drank this, I went to see the Customs Officer in my cabin.

"Any dope, drugs?" he asked casually.

"No."

"Rings, gold ones?"

"Only what I'm wearing."

"O.K. then."

And that was that. It seemed rather an incitement to smuggling, for I was unaware of the meticulous search, inspired by personal curiosity, of my property that lay ahead in Japan. I handed my passport and health certificates to the Purser and returned to the portrait of the Queen and my parents, silently pensive and awkward. Someone was talking in a loud unnatural voice. The constrained public atmosphere was as uncongenial to family farewells as the cold concrete and iron of the dock. At last I thought of showing my parents the cabin with its ingenious use of the small space. My mother insisted on unpacking some of my shirts.

Visitors were warned that they must soon leave the ship. "Mother," I said, at last coming to speak of what was in our hearts, remembering from talk in early years what tragedies happened to relations at home when others died abroad. "If I die out there and we never meet again, you must accept it as unavoidable and no worse than if it happened in England. I wouldn't want to think of you destroying yourself with a useless grief. And we shall meet again, some day."

"We shall meet again," she said firmly, accepting my words. My father looked on with approval. He would have to bear the brunt of my mother's sadness in the days to come, but I could not speak of what was the other fear—that should anything happen to either of them I would be helplessly at the other end of the world. There was numbness at my heart and we fell silent. We kissed goodbye.

"Don't stand too long and get pneumonia," I advised as they went down. "It's a terrible day." I had a premonition that as the Customs examination had been delayed, the ship's departure would be a lengthy affair and my mother, determined to see the ship beyond the horizon, might catch a death-cold at my departure as others at a grave-side.

Bit by bit the ship was freed from the quay, like the severing of other links, and moved shakily into the river. The other visitors had waved and were gone; the men who were working had all departed. Only the two figures were on the quay, small now, but my mother's green coat conspicuous as the Pharos fire. Infinitely slowly the ship slipped into the fog, and we stopped in the middle of nowhere. Then came slow, cumbersome manoeuvres as the ship took new directions. We advanced slowly again. The fog parted like the curtains of a theatre and I saw again the dock and the two tiny figures alone there. I blew a kiss and a green arm answered my signal. Then the fog closed and farewell was final.

EPILOGUE

We do not kill ourselves with work in this part of Japan. The miracle of Japan's economic prosperity—and the country is indeed prosperous—evidently comes from the efforts of other areas. Holidays abound; we are always having festivals. It is a festival today.

I am sitting in the garden. It has a Japanese pine, a haunting silhouette in the moonlight and an ever-changing, consolingly familiar, shape in the sunshine, a palm and other shrubs. There are some interestingly shaped and coloured rocks, and silver sand instead of grass. The dogs of the district are barking behind their walls, in an off-hand, sleepy way, as if they felt they should get their yap in before the noon comes. I am using the black and gold fan which my lover brought me from Kyoto. The mosquitoes are not out in the morning freshness and they seldom trouble me. But it is hot, even though I am in the light yukata or long-sleeved gown which is the only sensible informal wear here in the hot months.

Ken—a Japanese personal name as well as an English—should arrive on the noon train from Tokyo and he has arranged for us to see the Kabuki in the late afternoon. It is very seldom that there is a performance of the Kabuki theatre here. I have only been once before, with Mr. Takahara, and that time I nearly fainted with starvation as I had not expected the performance to be so long. This time I shall take some food. I want to take a bath before Ken comes, and it will be ready for him too, but there is time and it is pleasant to idle in the sunny solitude of the garden. I have not opened the letter from England, as I see it is from neither Jessie nor my mother, and strange letters fill me with a slight dread. They are more than likely to be from tax inspectors. But no tax official, if he used handwriting, would write like this. Feeling comfortable, I opened the letter.

"Dear Johnny," it began.

"We are in a crumby joint in Moss Side. We go to bed at seven every night and Frank keeps moaning that he could do with you here. He wants me to write and let you know how much he misses you, especially at bed-time. You should see the landlady here—a real tyke. She has had the gas cut off and the meter in the room emptied. I don't think she trusts us. She must have heard Frank wondering how much was in it.

"Frank had a good job driving for Willard Constructions but gave a bit of lip at the office, and I was given my cards for being a bit late. I wouldn't mind a night job, but the labour here is no good. Frank wants you to know that he is thinking of going to sea if he can find a ship touching Japan. It got a bit hot for us in Hawkward after we pasted Beggy's mug for him. He got nabbed for stealing a television set and Les Shaw is still inside, so if they're together I hope Les gives him another pasting.

"Frank wants to know if you have got a geisha. Have you got fixed up with someone in Japan?

"Johnny, we can't get the dole and there's nothing doing here. Frank sold the ring, for which thanks. He felt a bit of a sis wearing it. Do you think you could send us a bit of dough to tide us over? We wouldn't ask but we can't lay hands on the necessary. We haven't any contacts here. It wouldn't take more than a fortnight by air mail, but the sooner the better. We are in a right mess. Will you write to us at the post office and not here, as the old girl is dishonest enough to hold the letter for rent and we're not sure how long we'll be here?

Cheerio from me and Frank says lots of kisses.

Don."

"P.S. Alf is giving up the Whistle in Autumn. He can't stand it any longer with Evelyn in the pub, so he's moving to Scunthorpe to work in a steel factory."

This letter leaves me with a sharp feeling of irritation. It brings into my peaceful Japanese existence the unhappiness of old former things. I don't want to be mixed up with people who cannot keep at any sort of job. I am filled with panic at the thought of Frank coming to Japan. I have told Ken about Frank, but a former lover

112

present in the flesh is another matter, and I certainly don't intend to subsidise Frank's idling in Moss Side with Don. They must have obtained my address in Japan from a postman at Hawkward, I suppose. The best thing is for me to send no reply. I tear the letter up in resentment at being taken for granted and being jolted back into a past from which I thought I had escaped.

Well, I can't delay heating the bath, but as I do so, my resentment wears away. Frank with a criminal record would never obtain permission to settle in Japan and as a seaman he would officially not be allowed to travel very far from the ports, not that that would stop him. I know that he is likely to talk about coming to Japan but that will be as far as it will go. He will always remain Frank. Even if he did come I can be sure he would be tolerant and not jealous. I could prepare Ken gradually so that he wouldn't be jealous. But Frank will never come.

The words of Beggy have rankled with me ever since I heard them, but what truth was in them? Why should I believe Beggy against my own experience of Frank? I know well enough he is a weak character, but Beggy is vicious and probably attributed his own viciousness to Frank. I have paid too much heed to Beggy's words.

This calms me and I go out again to sit in the sun. It is better to let a Japanese bath cool to the right temperature rather than add cold water. I think of Frank at large in Moss Side. He's like a wild overgrown boy. Don is the one with *savoir faire*. I wonder what happened to his girl friend. The landlady is clearly not without her *savoir faire*.

If I don't send the money Frank will be in some trouble. If I do send the money he is just as likely to get into trouble. He is not likely to keep going to bed at seven for long.

A cloud is moving up to pass across the sun. A little black cat slips over the wall and in front of me hopefully examines the silver sand for traces of food. A black cat brings good luck in the North of England but bad luck in the South. I wonder what it is supposed to bring in Japan?

Well, I'll write a letter and send some money, but it will have to be tomorrow. The post office is closed. Today is a festival.

THE END